ONCE UPON A TIME IN MONTO

THE DARKLE CHRONICLES
BOOK TWO

B.C. HOLLYWOOD

Edited by 360 Editing (a division of Uncomfortably Dark). Editor: Candace Nola.
Cover by Don Noble of Rooster Republic Press

ISBN-13: 978-1068675720

WARNING

This book is an extreme horror story. It contains graphic depictions of violence, some SA references, and children in peril. Reader discretion is advised.

DARKLE DEFINITION

Dar-kle
1. To appear darkly or indistinctly.
2.
A. To grow dark.
B. To become gloomy.

CHAPTER I

DUBLIN 1888

Lorcan Crowley cut a menacing figure amid PS Violet's disembarking well-to-do passengers. He felt self-conscious of his unkempt appearance but quashed it whilst ignoring the many sidelong glances. Admittedly, he would benefit from a shave, a cut to his greying, shoulder-length hair, and for his once fine clothing, now well worn, to be set afire. If he was honest with himself, he knew he looked like a vagrant; no wonder respectable folk shied away. *A few moments more and I'll be free of these god-forsaken insects*, he thought.

The storm that had threatened throughout the crossing had just broken over the city and, laden with luggage, the weary travellers negotiated the rain slick gangway to North Wall Quay with care. Lorcan wasn't sorry to leave the paddle steamer behind; the passage from Holyhead to Dublin had been a rough bitch.

A bitter wind drove the downpour into the new arrivals, causing them to pull their coats and scarves closer. The lamps all along the quay shook and almost extinguished with each gust, their fitful light throwing strained faces into twisted masks.

Lorcan adjusted the leather bag at his shoulder as he continued to inch along the gangway. The bag's battered state stood in stark contrast to the pristine luggage around him. *Twenty years and this is all I come back with.*

Beside him walked a child of six, guided by her mother's hand. She stared at him, curiosity plain on her face in that way of youth. Lorcan winked at her. Of course, the girl's mother chose that moment to look his way. The woman's face transformed from mere plainness into something bitter, and she yanked the child out of Lorcan's reach.

Face like a bulldog licking piss off a nettle, he thought, but presented her with his most lecherous grin. Her attitude made his fingers itch for the kukri knife sheathed at his back, but he resisted the impulse. *Make it through the night, at least, without blood on your hands,* he admonished himself.

A final step brought him onto the quay, where he moved away from the stream of travellers. He halted ten yards from them to take a deep breath and exhale at a leisurely pace. The smells of the quays brought back vivid memories of his younger days, but he pushed them away, not ready for them yet. It was still a wonder he was back in Dublin. He'd sworn he'd never set foot in the place again. But even when he said it, all those years ago, he knew the lie of it. He had unfinished business there, and now that he was back, he wouldn't leave until he settled it.

From his first moments back, the city seemed much the same as when he'd departed, but his memory undoubtedly deceived him. This whore of a city had changed as much as he had, and likely not for the better. They had that much in common, this city and he.

Right at that moment, he had to decide on his next

course. He had planned on going straight to his old Dawson street residence, and sense told him to do so, but he couldn't face the place yet. *Not sober, anyway; too many memories.* So he stood there, the spray on his face, the sea air in his lungs, the flicker of gaslight chasing shadows across his face, and considered his options. At this hour, a man of disreputable character like him had only one destination. *Monto*, he thought.

Lorcan caught a whiff of his odour as he adjusted his bag on his shoulder. *First things first*, he thought, looking down at his sorry clothing. *I'll need some new rags.* He set off along the quay towards the city centre, eyes peeled for a man of his measurements.

LORCAN WATCHED the man approach along the quay from the direction of town. He was statue-still, a shadow among the shadows of Wapping Street, sizing up each passerby, having decided it would be easier to waylay someone in this locale.

The approaching man was a more dapper specimen than ideal, but for size, Lorcan wouldn't find a better match. Another half-dozen yards and he would fall into the man's tail as he passed. He'd pull the man into a side alley a few yards down.

Lorcan had stowed his belongings in a nook in the wall down the street, a stretch from his vantage point. He needed to be unfettered for the task at hand. He reached back to check that his kukri knife was ready for an easy drawing. The path to it remained unhindered and clear.

"What the fuck are ye doin' here?" came a hard voice, spiked with hostility, from behind Lorcan. He turned from the quay and his quarry to the shadows from which the voice had come. Only an Irish Mammy would love the face that greeted him; lumpy, scowling, and flinty-eyed. The man's physique was reminiscent of a solidly constructed shed.

"Dis is my street. What the hell are ye doin' here?" The Shed continued.

A pinch-faced stoat of a man peered from around The Shed. "Yeah. 'Tis our spot, like. Ye'll have ta pay us fer usin' it," said The Stoat.

They were a discordant duo, and Lorcan wondered at their commencement; at any other time, he might have inquired into it. But not this evening.

Lorcan drew the kukri. The sound of metal across leather whispered into the night. He lunged at The Shed aggressively, slashing out and embedding the top of the blade in the man's bull neck, half severing his head from his shoulders. The Shed dropped to his knees, reached up to claw away the blade, but his blood slicked hands couldn't find enough purchase on the knife to dislodge it. The Shed toppled forward, and planted his face on the cobblestones, nose pulping and teeth splintering upon impact.

At the first sign of violence, The Stoat squealed and dashed up Wapping Street without looking back.

So much for loyalty, thought Lorcan. He considered sending the kukri after The Stoat, but it was firmly lodged in The Shed's bull neck. It took a boot on the large man's head for leverage to open the wound enough to pull it clear. He cleaned it on The Shed's shirt before he sheathed it at his back again.

The big man wasn't as intimidating, lying dead in the gutter as he was. He wore an impressive black coat which had escaped the worst of the bloodshed. Lorcan grabbed one arm and kick-rolled the body out of it. *This'll do for now,* he thought, as he replaced his ragged coat with the freshly acquired one.

He retrieved his bag from its hiding place and continued towards Monto, his mood much improved upon. He smiled ruefully. *So much for making it through the night without bloodshed.*

CHAPTER 2
MONTO

Sebastian Renoir crouched in the doorway of the dilapidated Georgian house. Sheltered from rain and shadowed by the flickering lamplight, he watched a door across the cobbled street with a feverish intentness. He jerked his head violently at another whispered promise.

Soon, Sebastian. Soon.

"D'accord!" he said, too loud.

A street girl, passing at that moment, glanced his way, perhaps thinking him a potential customer. One brief impression was enough to hurry her away. Those reactions occurred more frequently of late. The fear and revulsion alarmed some part of him, hidden deep within, reflected in her retreating eyes. Before that inner voice could rise above a whimper, another whisper slid over it.

Concentrate!

Renoir adjusted his position to keep his line of sight with the door. For some unknown reason, he felt an intense need to do so, like it was a matter of life or death.

Despite the late October mizzle, Mecklenburg Street teemed with life; its denizens skittered here and there like insects exposed by a freshly lifted stone. The street itself lay at the heart of Monto, Dublin's infamous red-light district, the British Empire's grubbiest jewel. The rundown town-houses were once the homes of wealthy citizens, who had long since fled across the Liffey, or the Irish Sea, abandoning the area to the poor and decrepit. Entire families lived in a single room in many of the faded dwellings, while other buildings were re-appropriated as brothels or speakeasies.

However, those engaged in prostitution did not confine themselves to indoors. Mecklenburg and its adjoining streets were brimming with those who plied their trade and the ones who purchased. Many seekers of pleasure had already found what they had sought and returned home, lighter of pocket, conceivably satiated, potentially graced with infection or disease, but for others, the night's adventures had only begun.

Close by, a fine tart had hooked a gentleman, and they moved towards Renoir. The gentleman was in an advanced state of drunkenness.

"Come on then, dear. Let's have a taste before I buy."

He groped with enthusiastic aimlessness, to emphasise his words, but, with practiced ease, the whore sidestepped to safety.

"Coin first, if you don't mind, *sir*."

She took the gentleman by the arm and led him closer to the Frenchman's pocket of darkness. Her eyes drifted to her destination, and she halted, noticing the occupied space. Her lips parted as if to speak, and Renoir hoped she would approach so that he could release the darkness within his skull. But the whisper hissed a warning.

Unworthy, Sebastian. Soon!

Renoir directed a dagger'd look towards her, following

that tender line of sight, and felt satisfaction upon seeing the whore's eyes widen and her mouth lose its counterfeit smile.

"Not tonight," she said to the gentleman, and pushed him away. "It's late... I 'ave to be gettin' home."

With that, she disappeared into the crowd before the gentleman knew what had happened. He raised his hand towards where she had been but thought better of it and gave a small shrug. Plenty of tarts to tumble on the street that evening.

Renoir shifted his body and resumed his vigil. The girl he sought would be out soon. He could sense it. Then his night's pleasure would begin.

KATE O'CONNOR WASHED the day's grime from her body using a soaped-up cloth. She'd brought water from the kitchen half an hour past and, despite her bone-weariness, the damp heat on her skin felt pleasant. The feeling didn't last, and she hurried to complete her ablutions as a cold draft raised goosebumps, a taste of the winter to come, no doubt. Satisfied she was as clean as could be, Kate rinsed the cloth and went over her body again, wiping the film of soap and dirt away. She dried off and dressed in her ordinary clothes.

The day had been the busiest in months. She'd personally attended to the needs of thirteen gentlemen. *Thirteen*, she thought, *lucky for some*. She'd smiled for them, danced with them, laughed at their too clever jokes, drank enough to dull her senses, but not enough to earn a beating from Madam Arnott, and finish with a fumble and a fuck. Then on to the next.

She'd turned seventeen the past week, but her birthday had passed unnoticed. She didn't mind. There was little worthy of celebration. Working in the flash house this past year had dulled her senses and assigned her previous life to a dream-memory. She knew in her heart that she couldn't live this life for much longer. She felt old and numb. Summoning the will to go home felt nearly impossible.

Kate put on her heavy winter coat and left the second-floor bedroom, which served as a changing room for the flash house girls. On leaden legs, she descended the narrow staircase to the lower hallway and front door. Before even setting foot in the hallway, she felt the eyes of the house bully, Seamus, devour her. She did her best to ignore his hungry look. *No point in encouraging the poor eejit,* she thought, but she was terrified of insulting him. She knew a mean streak ran through that one's core.

Seamus unlatched the door, opened it, and poked out his head to gage the street's safety. Satisfied all was well, he opened the door wide enough to let her pass, but not so wide that she could avoid brushing against him. The sharp scent of stale sweat mixed with cheap whiskey repulsed her. He tried on a charming smile. "Safe home now, Kate."

"Aye, and sooner rather than later, Seamus." She stepped out into the night, gripping her coat close against the pelting rain. A few steps into the street and she heard the flash house door close behind her. She blended into the crowd as she crossed the shiny cobbles on her way to her room on Purdon Street. She lowered her head and ignored the surrounding bustle, intent on getting home.

As she traversed the street, her mind drifted back to the trouble which had landed her in this predicament. For the thousandth time, she cursed her drunkard father for selling her into this life to pay off his debts. "I hope you're rotting in some ditch, you useless excuse for a man!"

An approaching couple threw her an inquisitive look, and she dropped her head further, face colouring in embarrassment. Her sentiment did not change, though; she swore that if she escaped this life, she'd see that bollocks got his comeuppance.

Distracted by her musings, she turned right instead of keeping straight and entered the warren of narrow side streets lying between Mecklenburg and Purdon. She usually avoided this shortcut in the dark because the shadowed alleys drew the city's most desperate citizens, but she was tired and chanced taking it. The darkness enfolded her.

COAT CLUTCHED white-knuckle tight against the driving rain, Renoir strode down the whore-lined street. He gripped his curious staff, a twisted thing made of ash with a fist sized blackened stone atop. He wielded it as another man might wield a walking cane, tapping out his pace as he followed the girl. *TAP. TAP. TAP.*

The flicker of light from the streetlamps distorted the faces of passersby, so that twisted snarling lips accosted him from every side. *TAP. TAP. TAP.*

They offered their services unashamedly. "Two bob fer a ride, sir." Or, "The sweetest bush in Ireland, mister." Then they noticed his eyes and felt the menace emanate from him. A gasp, a stumble, an about-turn to flee, and a rough semi-circle of emptiness pushed ahead of him. *TAP. TAP. TAP.*

Renoir was oblivious. His fevered gaze remained locked upon the girl's slight form up ahead.

Almost! The insidious voice within his mind informed him.

The girl turned into the dense maze of alleyways a few yards' distance, and Sebastian hurried after. *TAP. TAP. TAP.*

TOMMY O'HARE WATCHED Mecklenburg Street from the meager shelter of an overhanging windowsill. His sister Margaret slumbered uneasily beside him. She was cold and damp, but at least he took the worst of the weather from her.

"No! Tommy, stop them!" called Margaret.

Tommy glanced down, saw that she was still asleep, and went back to his vigil. The nightmares came more often with the shortening of days. Nightmares or not, Tommy envied her slumber, but sleep wasn't for him yet; he had work to do. And if they wanted food in their bellies today, he'd better get to it. He scanned the street from left to right in search of a mark. *Someone old,* he thought, *a cattle trader, or a farmer. Some mucker from the country anyhow, in for a taste of what the city offers.* His eyes absorbed the street with greed. *Someone full of drink'd be nice; it'd be a cinch to rob them.* Tommy's slight frame shuddered, and his hand moved to his swollen face. *Not a soldier or sailor, anyway.*

Sharp pain lanced his ribs at the slight movement, and he grimaced. The young officer had caught him red-handed last night while liberating the coin from his pocket. Tommy had paid dearly for the mistake with a merciless beating that might have killed him had someone not intervened. He'd have to be more careful tonight.

Across the street, the door to the flash house opened and the bullhead of Seamus jutted out, looked around, and darted in again. Then Kate stepped out, and without a backward glance, hurried away. Seamus, the house bully, mooned after her before shutting the door. *Feckin' eejit*, thought Tommy.

Tommy liked Kate; she looked out for him and his sister, made sure they had food when pickings were slim, and always had a generous smile and a "Hello" whenever she saw them. Not like most hereabouts, some would sooner spit on you as look at you.

As he followed Kate's progress, he noticed movement at the periphery of his vision. A man, who had been hunched down in a nearby doorway, moved in the same direction as her. Instinctively, Tommy knew the man was in pursuit. Well versed in the art of staying hidden, he knew a tail when he saw one. He studied the man more closely, or tried to, but the man seemed to gather the shadows about himself. *If it's a man at all!*

Tommy found it impossible to get a bead on the shadow-man. His eyes just slid off him as though Tommy's inner Peeler said, "Nothing to see here," and moved him away from the scene of some interesting crime. As the shadow-man approached Tommy, he heard the tap-tapping of his cane. *TAP. TAP. TAP.* A dull, rhythmic sound, like nails being driven into a coffin. A sound that Tommy could follow. "Margaret!"

His sister's eyes shot open. "What?" She got her bearings and in her little voice said, "Jaysus, Tommy. Ye frightened the life out of me!"

"Kate's in trouble. We have to help." One thing Tommy knew for certain was the shadow-man held no good intentions for Kate. He gripped his sister's arm and raced after the tap-tapping.

TAP. TAP. TAP. Renoir was about to follow the girl into the warren of alleyways when a pair of sodden street children stumbled into his path. The older of them, a boy with a swollen face, held out his filthy hands in an aspect of supplication.

"Spare a farthing, mister? It's been days since we 'et."

Renoir glared at them. The desire to obliterate their pathetic forms was overwhelming, but he couldn't spare the seconds required for such satisfaction. *There'll be time for minor pleasures later,* he thought.

Yes!, agreed the voice.

He knocked the boy and his smaller companion to the gutter with a savage blow from his staff and strode on. *TAP. TAP. TAP.*

With no time to spare, he turned into the alley in time to glimpse the girl vanishing around the distant corner. He picked up his pace, eager now that he was so close. *TAP. TAP. TAP.*

CHAPTER 3

MAGIC AND MAYHEM

Lorcan stepped out of the síbín onto Lower Mecklenburg Street, feeling as sober as when he'd stepped in an hour and a half ago, despite the fair swallow of liquor he'd partaken of. Then the cold air hit his lungs, causing his head to swim dangerously. *Perhaps I'm further along than I thought.*

He lifted his coat lapels against the rain and was deciding his next destination when a pair of children jostled into him, causing him to lose his balance. The smaller of the two, a young girl who looked to be around eight, offered a quick 'sorry' before continuing on her way. Bemused, Lorcan watched them. The boy, who appeared to be around ten years old, kept glancing anxiously behind him. Lorcan followed his gaze to a man in a tailcoat, top hat, and billowing cloak, who carried an odd-looking cane with a dark stone on its handle. The intensity of the man's gaze stood out. That and how the crowded street yielded to him. *How curious,* he thought.

The youngsters stopped in the strange man's path and, when he was almost upon them, the boy stepped in his way, colliding hard with him. Lorcan assumed the boy was a pickpocket, but the boy surprised him by showing no interest in stealing the man's purse.

The strange man viciously struck the children down to the street. Lorcan winced at the savagery, noting the boy's damaged face for the first time. *He's no stranger to violence.* It reminded Lorcan of himself at that age. Despite suspecting that the nostalgia and the drink were influencing him, he decided to find out what was happening. He approached the pair and offered his hand. "He's a strange one," said Lorcan, to break the ice.

The boy looked at the proffered hand as if it might bite, then studied Lorcan's eyes for signs of ill intent. Evidently satisfied, the boy accepted the help. "You've got to stop him, mister!" the boy burst out as Lorcan helped his companion up. "He's after Kate!"

Lorcan looked about for the strange man and spotted his distinctive top hat disappear into a side alley a few yards up the street.

"Please help her, mister," said the girl.

He looked at their pleading faces, then back to the alley. He did not know what they were involved with, or who this Kate was, but the strange man smelled dangerous to Lorcan. And he thought danger might be just what he needed to take his mind off his return. "Alright. I'll help her." He handed them his bag. "You two mind this... and stay here."

They looked at one another, then nodded in unison. Satisfied, Lorcan set off after the strange man.

Renoir closed the distance between himself and the girl. He raised the staff to quit the tap-tapping for stealth's sake and, with a last burst of speed, bore down on his quarry. He halted close enough to smell her sweet perfume and inhaled deeply.

The girl, hearing his breath in the alley's stillness, tripped over herself in her haste to turn. Her eyes made wide circles in the gloom. "You!" she said.

Before she could make another sound, he shoved her head into the alley's solid wall. The impact rocked her. Her eyes lost their focus. Renoir used her confused state and, with a vice-like grip, dragged her to a secluded yard formed by the chance meeting of three rough walls. The stench of rotting garbage hung heavily in the air, despite the attempts to mask it with ash.

The odour did not bother Renoir. It mattered not a ha'penny for the work at hand. He produced a knife from beneath his coat - a vicious, double-edged piece - and used it to strip the girl. His motions were fluid and practiced, and moments later she lay exposed on a bed of shredded garments. The drizzle formed a glistening layer on her pale skin. She shivered. Her head moved and a weak moan escaped her. She would be conscious soon and Renoir was determined his timing would be on the mark. He set to work.

With a steady hand, he slashed symbols into her soft flesh, on her belly, her breasts, her thighs, and as he did so spoke a guttural incantation. He barked the words at the night as the rain intensified. Far in the distance, thunder rolled. Still speaking, he dropped the knife and lay his left hand on her stomach with the fingers splayed. His right hand held tight to his staff. The blackened stone pulsed.

The girl's eyes opened wide and locked onto his. Renoir

knew she wanted to scream, to fight, to flee - anything but lie there helpless as she did. Tears pooled at the corners of her eyes, leaked out, and flowed down her face as sistered streams. She looked at the pulsing stone, then to her stomach, attracted by other movements. His fingers shed their shape and transformed into fleshy tendrils, stretching across her belly in search of the cuts he'd made. They squirmed across her and inside her body, deeper and deeper. The penetration was exquisite for him.

Renoir's voice boomed out, louder than before, and his face distorted, caught in the region betwixt pleasure and pain. Thunder rolled again, closer. Thin tendrils of steam drifted from the finger-holes and the faint smell of corrupted flesh permeated the air. Renoir's body tensed.

On his staff, the blackened stone grew richer, plumper, to resemble a fleshy heart. It gave one strong beat, another. Renoir, rigid in the last moments of the ritual, relaxed and allowed himself to breathe. The girl slumped lifelessly beneath him. The stone was bereft of life again. *It is done.*

Renoir didn't know if that was his own thought or the other's. He removed fingers slick with clotting blood from the girl. They were ordinary human digits again, and he wiped them clean as best he could on her tattered petticoat. He looked at her lying there, twisted and bloodied and pale, beautiful in death, and he felt a stirring. The contrast of scarlet blood splashed on milky skin was striking, and the fine blond 'v' of pubic hair hardly concealed the pink delight beneath. The red mist of desire descended upon him. Laying his staff to one side, Renoir loosened his belt, unfastened his breaches, and moved onto the slow-cooling corpse, a different sort of penetration on his mind.

~

"WHAT VILE SHIT IS THIS?" Lorcan had seen plenty of twisted happenings in his life, but what he witnessed in the ash-pit dump made his stomach heave and threaten to spill the night's drinking on the ground.

A devil moved atop the naked body of a young woman. It grunted as it rutted like a beast of the field. The poor girl's eyes, glazed in death, stared through Lorcan, or into the depths of him. With each violent thrust her lolling head shifted, or a limb moved, in mimicry of life. Surely this devil used her more wickedly in death than she'd experienced in life.

Lorcan stood frozen at the yard's entrance, but the devil had noticed him. Its movement ceased, and the devil slow-turned towards him. The creature's eyes were black wells trying to swallow him. It flicked out a tongue to slurp blood from its lips, then twisted its mouth in a smile wide with insanity.

Before Lorcan could react, there came a cry of rage from behind him. "No!" Then a blur of movement. The boy from the street hurtled past, bent on attack. But the devil was too quick. Lorcan couldn't believe how quick. It dismounted the corpse and turned in time to grab the boy by the throat with one hand, lifting him high. As it strangled him, it reached its free hand for the strange staff which lay close by.

Lorcan, a long-time practitioner of the art of self-preservation, knew in situations such as this offense was often the best defense. While the devil was distracted, he sped in and picked up the staff. He hefted it as he stepped back and, satisfied by the weight, lifted the heavy piece of wood over his shoulder.

"Tommy!" It was the boy's companion, the little girl.

She stepped into the waste-ground, wide-eyed and open-mouthed, walking hesitantly to Tommy. *Stupid child!*

With no time to lose, Lorcan swung the weapon in a wide arc. Before the devil could react, the heavy end crashed into its head. The force sent the devil flying into a filth strewn corner, leaving Tommy to drop to the ground and suck in much needed air.

Lorcan thought he'd heard the devil's skull crack, but wasn't taking any chances. He set to work on the devil's body, pummelling it from toes to crown. If the devil awoke, it would only have broken bones to rise upon.

Minutes passed as Lorcan administered the beating until he felt satisfied the task was complete. He stepped back and leaned against the wall. He breathed heavily and a film of sweat mixed with the rain had formed on his skin. Only then did he notice the children staring at him.

There was an awkward silence, broken by the boy, Tommy. "Is it dead?"

Lorcan nodded.

Tommy approached the beaten devil, his little companion in toe, and spat on it. "What was he doin' to her?"

Lorcan heard the edge in the boy's voice. The girl whimpered. He felt it wasn't the time to inform them about the birds and the bees. "Only him and Auld Nick know that." Lorcan pushed himself away from the wall and collected his bag from where the girl had dropped it. He nodded to the bodies. "Take what you can, then get away from here." Lorcan shouldered his bag, and double timed it out of there. He was scarcely aware that he still held onto the devil's staff.

~

WITH GREAT RELIEF, Tommy led Margaret through the front door of the tiny ramshackle house on Beaver Street. They lived in a back room with other destitute children; some who were orphans like them and some who were Monto Babies, children given up by prostitute mothers. Slumbering forms dotted the floor, but they found a relatively dry spot against the back wall with only the occasional drip of rainwater from the ceiling. Straight away, the cold and damp seeped into Tommy. The heat brought on by the dash home wore off, and the shock of what he'd witnessed shook him all over. He looked at Margaret. "Are you okay?"

She nodded but wouldn't meet his eyes. He'd taken the man's advice and searched poor Kate and the devil for coin and valuables. He'd crossed himself before apprehensively checking the devil's corpse, making a pile on a piece of Kate's torn dress, then he searched Kate, avoiding the blood where he could, and added the pittance he found on her to the pile. As he'd twisted the ragged cloth into a makeshift bag and tied it tight, Margaret had covered Kate's nakedness with the shredded remnants of her clothing. When she'd done what she could, she threw a frosty look at the cloth bundle in Tommy's hand.

He'd shrugged. "Better in our pocket than someone else's." Then they'd got out of there like the devil himself was at their back; Tommy supposed he was.

The boy shivered at the memory.

"Did somebody walk over your grave, Tommy?" asked Margaret.

"Yeah." He pulled her close to him. "Come on. Get some rest." But where Margaret effortlessly fell into the rhythm of sleep, Tommy found that devil leering back at him each time he closed his eyes.

CHAPTER 4
SISTERS OF CHARITY

Picture the Void. Dark, but not just darkness; the absence of everything, including light. Not just cold, not even cold, but no temperature. Nothingness... but that term still implies space. Unknowable, that may suit for now. The Void exists in the crack between universes, a place of transit, a buffer zone, a place where anything might be lost.

A place of Exile.

Into this place, or idea, or absence, come two thoughts; disembodied projections of mind, the only form of sentience that may enter here. They are ancient beings, the creatures from which these two minds originate, older than those found in most universes, and they have come here to confer.

The key is nearing full charge.

That is good news. Some doubted your commitment to our cause.

I am offended, Brother.

As you wish. Just ensure that you perform the ritual soon. Rumours are rife with plans to replace you.

The time draws nearer with each use. Soon, Brother.

How soon?

What is Time to us who have waited countless eons? Another century, another millennium, would be inconsequential.

As you say, time holds little meaning for us. Mark this though, if another century passes, you will not be around to see it. Now *is your time, Little Sister.*

The disdain in the moniker, 'Little Sister', was not lost on the other, but the bait was not taken.

I appreciate your candour, Brother. Thank you.

Thank me with deeds. Our Lord is eager to feel the ground wasting beneath him once more. And it has been long since we have tasted flesh...

It will be soon. You have my word, Brother.

Good. I must leave you then. Much work lies ahead.

For us all.

The thoughts dissipate and The Void, silent once more, breathed an airless sigh of regret.

DEEP within the Convent of the Sisters of Charity on Gloucester Street, the Mother Superior sat hunched within a circle of protection drawn upon the stone slabbed floor of the ritual chamber. Her white habit's voluminous cowl threw her face into shadow. A face encased in the onyx mask which denoted her station as head of the convent. Her chest moved in a smooth inhale, exhale, of breath; a casual observer might think she slept.

An immense mirror graced the wall before her, a swirling inkiness held by an ornate frame which was carved from a single piece of ancient timber. Only her order knew of the object's origin. To stare too long into its black depths was to risk an endless falling. Those brave souls who had dared to do so had been consumed entirely.

The Mother abruptly stiffened, and her breathing halted in a harsh rasp. Nothing but stillness for an agonised moment. Then she exhaled tremulously, relaxed her body, and opened her eyes. The two orbs glowed red from behind the mask within the cowl. She moved her limbs a little at a time to become accustomed to her mortal coil again, musing that it felt much like surfacing from a deep sleep.

The Mother's thoughts were a swirl, troubling her. Those who waited beyond the gate were dissatisfied with the pace of her work and now, of all times, they wished to force her hand. This angered her. They spoke of the key as though it was tangible, disregarding its intricate combination of ancestral lineages and current circumstances. *Fools!*

She knew who the staff was with, if not their exact location. She had placed it with the Frenchman herself and he fed it as it... changed him. The second part of the puzzle, an old bloodline from this isle, was safe in the Order's countryside convent. But doubt niggled at her.

She reached outside the circle and retrieved a silver bowl and decanter of clear liquid, long claw-like nails clacking off metal and glass. She opened the decanter and half-filled the bowl with liquid, then pulled up the sleeve of her habit to expose an emaciated arm. A flick of a fingernail opened a cut from which she squeezed drops of something darker and thicker than blood into the bowl. She swirled the liquid around with the same fingernail and the liquid turned black as midnight.

With the bowl held close, she focused her mind on the image of Sebastian Renoir. After a while, shapes formed, but no single image took hold. *Strange...* Renoir had an exceptionally twisted mind which should have stood out in the city like a dark insect scuttling over fresh paper. *Maybe not* fresh *paper,* she thought. *Dublin is more like an old pamphlet lying in the gutter.*

The image pleased her, and a laugh grated from deep inside. It fast faded. The bowl unveiled a scene of death, with Renoir its central subject. She leaned closer, red orbs consuming the scene. Of the staff, there was no sign, and she cursed his incompetence. She had thought him cunning enough to protect it. She attempted to expand the scene, but it proved futile. Desperation crept over her.

She swirled the inky liquid around quickly, and the scene dissipated. Within her mind, she focused on the girl, Fea Murrigan. A new scene formed within the bowl, and The Mother gasped. Fea was in a dilapidated barn or shed, surrounded by a group of men who closed upon her. The girl was terrified.

The Mother threw the bowl aside, spraying the dark liquid across the stone floor, the bowl clattering to a halt beside the wall. *Damn you!* Even she wasn't sure who she cursed; the Sisters tasked with watching the girl, the men who accosted her, or the fool girl herself for getting into such a predicament. "Sister!" she called.

A Sister glided into the room to the sound of a dying breath, her hands concealed within the sleeves of her habit, pale orbs glowing from within the white porcelain mask beneath her cowl. "Yes, Mother?"

The Mother pointed to the bowl, where the image was gradually becoming less distinct. "Contact our country Sisters and find out what happened with the Murrigan girl."

"Yes, Mother," said the Sister and turned to leave.

"And Sister?"

The Sister paused in her turn. "Yes, Mother?"

"Locate the Frenchman and return with the staff. And take care of the mess he's made."

"As you command, Mother."

The Sister bowed and left The Mother to silence and dark thoughts. She had journeyed for what felt like an eternity, and it would be over her desiccated carcass they would usurp her now.

THE SISTER, wearing a hooded cloak over her habit to conceal The Order's involvement, studied the bloody scene in silence. She sniffed at the air inquisitively, moving first to the sorcerer and then to the prostitute's broken body. She pulled away the shredded garments and examined the symbols carved into her pallid corpse. *The runes are correct...* she thought.

She leaned closer to the glistening wounds and inhaled deeply, the metallic scent of blood filling her nostrils. A long, discoloured tongue curled from the darkness of her hood and into the holes, savouring each. *The ritual was successful...*

Sinking to all fours, she moved close to the corpse's sex organ. She sniffed again, one long inhalation, then moved her probing tongue around the edge and into it, tasting. *Interesting...* The girl's sex organ was torn, so the Sister surmised the sorcerer gave in to his baser instincts. But only after the ritual completed, and the girl had died. *Foolish.*

She dismissed the prostitute and stood, tongue disappearing into her dark hood as she returned to the sorcerer. Apart from the clothing, he was almost unrecognisable. *Who could do this to him?* No matter. The harm was done. She had a more pressing matter to attend to.

She circled out from the sorcerer's body, scanning the ground for signs of the staff. It didn't take long to cover the small yard, but the staff was nowhere to be seen. However, indications of recent human activity were present.

She would report her findings to The Mother upon her return to the convent. If not weighed down by more misfortune, the Mother would offer guidance. Their country Sisters' answer to the question about the Murrigan girl had displeased The Mother greatly. The girl had escaped from their country convent over a week ago, but they had been assured that a pair of Sisters closed in on Fea and would have her soon. *For their own good, they better.* It wouldn't surprise her if The Mother razed the country convent to the ground, with all the Sisters still inside if they didn't deliver on that promise.

Before the Sister left the murder scene, she cleansed the area. With unusual strength, she lifted the prostitute's body onto a hand cart brought for such use, then deftly placed the sorcerer on top. She covered the load with a tarpaulin and tied it down.

The Sister took one last look around to be sure she'd missed nothing. Satisfied, she lifted the handcart's handles and wheeled it towards the convent. The walls could easily accommodate the disposal of the likes of them.

THE GARDEN, tucked away in the grounds of the convent, was empty apart for the Sister toiling in the shallow grave.

Satisfied at the depth, she placed the spade to one side and climbed out. She looked around at the seeded beds and mused that it would soon be necessary to choose another location for such necessary work. *The Mother will guide us,* she thought and turned back to the task at hand.

She tipped the contents of the handcart onto the rain-damp grass, causing the stench of putrefying flesh to waft over her. She breathed deeply to fill her lungs with it. Accelerated decay was a known side effect of dark magic and one of her personal favourites.

Conscious of the time, and that the women of The Laundry would soon be about their duties, the Sister set about concluding the morning's work. She stripped the prostitute of tattered garments and dumped her into the shallow grave. She repeated the process on the sorcerer. Their nakedness would ease the transition from flesh to soil. A few minutes of shoveling saw the bodies concealed by muddy earth in readiness for seeding later in the day. Come spring, she expected an abundance of blooms.

She gathered up the clothing and placed it in the handcart. She set off towards the furnace. After the incineration was done, she could breathe a sigh of relief knowing that she had fulfilled her duty to The Mother. Approaching the convent proper, she felt strange, and it took her a moment to place the feeling. *Am I nervous?* Yes. That was it. The Sister felt nervous; not a feeling she was accustomed to. Others usually felt nervous when Sisters were around. But the circumstances were extenuating. *The staff,* she thought. *The Mother will be displeased upon learning of its absence.*

The Sister continued her walk towards the convent proper, her stomach in knots. She dreaded the coming confrontation with The Mother.

"THE SORCERER IS DECEASED, MOTHER," said the Sister.

The Mother greeted the news with a silence that stretched into minutes. She felt the fear emanating from her underling, but on the surface, the Sister showed no emotion. The Mother respected that and fought to control her rage. "How?"

"Someone murdered him. Pummelled to death," said the Sister, adding, "while in coitus."

A curse upon the carnality of man, thought The Mother. "And the Staff?"

"Of the Staff there was no sign, Mother."

The Mother used another spate of silence to reign in her anger. She had expected as much, else the Sister before her would have given her the staff already. "That is... unfortunate."

"Yes, Mother."

The Mother had to maintain composure in front of her subordinate, despite the unfavourable circumstances. She marvelled at the way her meticulously crafted plans unravelled, yet took it as a sign that her path was true. "This world conspires against us," she said, almost to herself.

"Conspires against us, Mother?"

The Mother ignored the Sister. She hadn't meant to vocalise her thoughts; she was too long living within the realm of humanity. It was time for the world to turn against itself. "Release the hound, Sister."

"Is that wise, Mother?"

The Mother's eyes turned to twin furnaces and blazed from beneath her onyx mask. "Wiser than questioning me."

The Sister bent in supplication. "I meant nothing of it, Mother."

"Do as I bid you. Release the hound."

The Sister remained bent low as she retreated backwards from the room, but the damage had been done. The Mother couldn't believe the Sister's audacity and vowed to choose another First as soon as this was over.

CHAPTER 5
OLD HAUNTS

Feed...

The townhouse on Dawson Street was cold. Lorcan gripped the staff tightly as he stood in the entrance hall, soaked through from his journey from Monto. He barely noticed his sodden state, transfixed as he was by the unfamiliar feel of a place once so familiar.

...feed...

The past's echoes told him that his son, Cormac, should have hurtled down the stairs and into his arms by now. In the distant past, his return from a lengthy absence would see him fending off a barrage of questions, the boy's curiosity and enthusiasm bringing an amused shake to Lorcan's head.

...feed...

His wife, Nemhain, would appear then, from within the depths of her study, where she spent most of her days immersed in stories or penning her own. She would greet him with an amiable smile and reward his return with a playful peck on the cheek. That was before the darkness stole her smiles away.

...feed...

It occurred to Lorcan, as he stood dripping in the hallway, that his memories of his life in the house could have been a wonderful dream, and now, back in the waking world, this empty place could not compete with his fantasy. The absence of his family was a hollow place within him and again he pondered the cruelty inherent in life. It was impossible for him to comprehend now. Over twenty years ago, his wife and son had been alive and breathed life into these halls and rooms. Now it felt like he stood within a tomb.

...feed...

He removed the massive coat, now soaked through, and hung it upon an empty hook on the wall. The sight of the shoe rack beneath the hook made him pause. He recalled a pair of small shoes sitting next to his own and felt his legs weaken. More memories of his old life came to him and threatened to overwhelm him with a thousand tiny details of what he had once taken for granted. He let the memories come; he accepted them. For twenty years he had fought them down, buried them in a sea of excess. He had done whatever it took to take his mind from thoughts of Nemhain and Cormac, but he was done running from their ghosts. He sighed and felt an overwhelming sense of relief. It would be over soon.

...feed...

Shut up, damn you! The whispers began in Monto not long after his confrontation with that devil. They'd grown more and more incessant ever since. Initially, he mistook it for the wind whistling through the narrow gaps between the buildings. Then he thought it might be the rustling of the leaves or the sound of a discarded newspaper being tossed around by the wind. But each time, the message was the same.

...feed...

With each whisper he felt an increase in purpose and soon a curious tingling sensation began in the hand gripping the staff. By the time he'd crossed the river, it had traveled up his arm, across his shoulder, and up the nape of his neck into his skull. The hair felt as though it stood on end.

...feed...

The whisper requested something trivial; all that was required of Lorcan was to agree and the pact could be made. *What would you have me feed upon?*

The servant's return broke Lorcan's rumination. The man's expression was more dour than when he'd answered Lorcan's knock minutes earlier, if that was possible. Lorcan had wedged his foot in the door, preventing it from closing, and firmly stated his name and that he wanted to speak with the master of the house. The servant had begrudgingly allowed Lorcan to wait in the entrance hall as he relayed the request.

"I'm afraid you'll have to be leaving," the servant informed Lorcan.

Everything about the man rubbed Lorcan up the wrong way; the dismissive tone, the hint of a satisfied smile at relaying his master's message, the way he looked down his nose at Lorcan despite being half a head shorter. And all under Lorcan's own roof? The rage boiled to the surface.

...feed...upon...HIM...

"Show me," said Lorcan. Before he could retract, the staff sent a wave of energy into his arm. *WHUMP.* As the energy moved to the shoulder, across his back, and into the opposite arm, Lorcan closed the distance between himself and the servant. Quicker than a cornered snake, Lorcan's hand shot out and caught the servant by the throat. He guided the squealing man down the hall, away from the front door. As he did so, the wave crested in a tingling sensation to his fingertips.

WHUMP. Another wave flowed into him. A small part of Lorcan protested, wanted to cease whatever this was before it was too late, but mostly he rejoiced in the power coursing through him. An inky blackness flowed over his pupils as his fingertips lengthened and sank into the servant's neck, cutting off his air supply.

WHUMP. The darkness smothered the tiny light inside Lorcan, and its death was a revelation. For the first time in years, the pain of loss was alleviated. Not gone. He could still sense it within him, but it no longer crushed him beneath its impossible weight.

WHUMP. The waves of energy continued and with each one, his fingers sank deeper into the servant's flesh. He felt the sensation of them squirming deeper.

WHUMP. It infused Lorcan with strength, and all the aches of age fell away from him. It was no effort to lift the servant, nor did the man's suffocating jig against the wall make the slightest difference.

WHUMP. His finger-tentacles pulsed as something vital of the servant was sucked through Lorcan and into the staff. And like that, it was over. Lorcan dropped the diminished body to the floor and went to explore his old abode.

Lorcan climbed the stairs to the upper floor. He knew precisely where the master's study was, for it had once been his own. First door on the left from the top of the stairs. He saw the yellow strip of light at the bottom of the door; confirmation that the room was the correct one.

...feed...

You can't still be hungry, thought Lorcan, as he pushed the whispered demand down and *tap-tapped* on the study door.

"Come in," said an impatient voice from within.

Lorcan opened the door and entered. The study was as he remembered it. His writing desk was still next to the ceiling-high window to take full advantage of the natural light. Of course, a new master sat behind it. The man didn't look up.

"Is the scoundrel gone?" the master of the house asked.

Lorcan remained silent but closed the door carefully behind him. Lorcan had never seen this man before, but judging by his youth, that was no mystery; the man would have been a child when Lorcan last set foot in the house.

The final click of the door informed the master that something was amiss. When he raised his head to find Lorcan instead of the expected manservant, it rendered him speechless.

He recognises me, though.

It took but a moment for the master to find his voice. "It can't be! You're dead!"

Lorcan looked down at himself in mock surprise. "Evidently not," he said, approaching the desk. With great deliberateness, he rested a foot on a chair opposite the man, then leaned his forearm on that leg and drew his kukri. He went about scraping the congealed blood from beneath his fingernails. The man could have been hypnotised, so entranced was he.

Lorcan blew off the residual flakes of blood, satisfied

the nails were clean. He began on the other. "Who are you?" he asked.

The hypnotised man jumped at Lorcan's question. Then he bit his lip as though deliberating an answer.

Lorcan continued scraping clean his fingernails.

The man straightened; he came to a decision. "I'm the master of this house. Cormac Crowley," he declared.

The scraping halted and Lorcan raised his head, looking the man who was not his son dead in the eye. "You are Cormac Crowley?"

Without hesitation, the man responded, "Yes."

Does he even see the lie in it? Lorcan wondered.

At that moment, a tiny figure dashed into the office. "Daddy!" The girl was no more than seven years of age, by Lorcan's estimate. She wore a dressing gown and looked as though she had been in bed.

"Not now, Rose," said the man. Lorcan couldn't think of him as Cormac. Whether or not intentionally, the man was an affront to his son's memory. He and whoever else was responsible would pay for that.

The girl ignored her father's instruction. "But Daddy, I had such a funny dream."

"I'm busy, Rose. You can tell me all about it later."

Lorcan detected a strained tone in the man's voice. His daughter's intrusion had placed him on edge.

The girl turned her attention to Lorcan. She wrinkled her nose at his unkempt state. "Who are you?"

"Hello, Rose. I'm Lorcan. An old friend of the family." He shone her a winning smile.

"Pleased to meet you, Lorcan," she said, and graced him with a little curtsy.

His smile broadened, and he raised his eyebrows at the man in appreciation of the girl's manners. It was a rare thing nowadays. The man, however, had grown more uncomfortable, acutely aware of the knife in Lorcan's hand. *Such a darling child,* thought Lorcan. He almost felt guilty about what he was about to do. "Do you love your daddy, Rose?"

"Yes," she replied, but a frown creased her brow.

"Would you rather live while your daddy died? Or would you prefer to die with him?"

"Stop this!" said the man, eyes wide with terror.

Lorcan pointed at the man with his kukri. "Let her answer!"

Tears brimmed in the child's eyes and her bottom lip trembled.

"Let me repeat the question, sweetheart. Would you rather live while your daddy died? Or would you prefer to die with him?"

Rose looked to her father for support, but he was watching Lorcan like he watched a wild animal. The floodgates broke, and she said with a sob. "I'd prefer to die with my daddy." She ran into his arms and the man held her close.

"No!" said the man, close to tears himself.

Lorcan's voice was icy. "Your daughter shows more strength of character than you do." Lorcan looked at the girl.

"Run along now, Rose. Your daddy and I have business to attend to."

Seeing the opportunity open, the man encouraged her. "Go on now, Rose. Go to Aunt Catherine."

Lorcan followed the child to the door, closing it after her. Something the man had said to the child sparked a memory. A tingling sensation began in his fingers as he turned to the man who said he was his son.

...feed...

"Tell me about Aunt Catherine."

CATHERINE O'SULLIVAN STOOD in the entrance hall, a slight frown on her brow. The large black coat, dripping all over the clean floor, drew her attention. She'd ventured downstairs to investigate the late-night caller. She was in an irritable mood; as the house mistress, she should have been informed of visitors. Instead, the sound of unfamiliar voices had roused from her slumber. Mattie should have known better, and he'd feel her wrath before the night was out. She gave a *tsk* at the impertinence, followed by a bellow. "Mattie!"

Moments passed with no sign of Mattie, and after several minutes more spent scowling at the monstrous black thing, hanging there, dripping, she pulled it from the hook and dumped it on the floor. Clutching her dressing gown close, she strode back into the house, intent on hunting the wayward servant down. Her eyes burned with fury, foreshadowing the man's regret when she found him. "Mattie!"

She marched down the hall towards the kitchen. Halfway to the kitchen door, her foot caught on something, almost causing her to tumble. "Jesus, Mary, and Joseph!" she said, thinking, *I'll kill that feckin' eejit when I get him.* Then she copped the feckin' eejit lying on the floor. At first, she thought he had lost all sense and was drunk, but then she saw the state of him. But for the familiar clothing she wouldn't recognize him, face wrinkled and drawn, mouth agape in horror. *What in God's name happened to him?*

Coldness ran through her, a companion to the horror

she felt. The last number of days had an ominous taint, but she'd put it down to the time of year. The anniversary of the old mistress's death approached, and it always affected her mood. She hadn't liked the woman at all. It seemed to Catherine that she had ideas above her station that marrying the master had brought into reality. The truth of her mood shift was that if ever they'd be discovered, it would be at this time of year.

"Auntie!" Panic froze her to the spot, but she spun out of it to face the child, shielding her from Mattie's body. She needn't have worried; Rose was in such a state that if there'd been ten bodies stacked one atop the other, she wouldn't have noticed.

Catherine led the child back towards the front of the house. "Calm down, Rose. What is it?"

Rose gasped for breath between words. "Auntie... scary... man... with... Daddy..."

The girl was descending into hysterics, but Catherine couldn't let her. She took her by the shoulders and gave her a firm shaking. The shock of the unexpected violence brought the child out of it, so Catherine continued. "What scary man?"

Rose's eyes were shocked wide, but she answered clearly. "The scary man with Daddy. His name is Lorcan. He asked me if I wanted to die with Daddy!" The child was off again, over the edge and likely that way for a while.

Catherine hardly noticed. The sound of that name hung in the air like a death knell to her machinations. *Lorcan.* The child had to be taken care of first. She was, after all, her only grandchild, though very few knew it. "Rose! Come!" Catherine grabbed her by the hand and they both ran headlong out the front door.

CATHERINE STOLE BACK into the house, alert to any noise that might hint at her son's fate. She hadn't been gone long; just enough time to see Rose safe in a neighbor's house on a hastily constructed pretense. *Please be okay, Cormac,* she thought, then corrected herself. *Liam! Please be okay, Liam!* She'd lived with the lie for twenty years and she was loath to live with it any longer. What had spurred her to do as she did? She still didn't know, after all these years. She had seen an opportunity in a time of chaos and had acted.

Mattie was as she'd left him, a crumpled body in the hallway. *Poor Mattie,* she thought. He'd been with her through it all.

She moved to the stairs and, choosing her steps to avoid the creaks and groans, she ascended. Her neck strained upwards, but there was no sign of movement above.

It can't really be him, can it? It hadn't been her fault when that witch, Nemhain, had drowned herself and her little fella. Nor was she to blame for the Master's dark spirit. He'd left them all high and dry when he'd vanished before they had buried the witch. When the boy's body hadn't surfaced, she'd jumped at the chance to secure her own future. She installed her son in little Cormac's place and herself as his guardian. A bold move, but nobody had batted an eye.

She paused at the top of the stairs to listen. A strange sucking noise came from down the hall. She lifted her dressing gown and pulled a wicked looking straight razor from its folds. She opened it in a grip for striking. Crouching outside her son's study, she peered through the keyhole. She couldn't make out anything, but the wet sucking noise came from within. "Cormac?" she called, in little more than a whisper.

Deep down, she was sure the Master was back and was no doubt full of questions. Well, Catherine had all the answers he'd need. She switched the straight razor to her other hand and tried the door handle. The door was unlocked, so she forcefully pushed it open. "Liam!"

All her pretense dropped from her as she took in the scene. She didn't understand what was happening to her son. He lay arched back over the large desk with his head hanging over the edge. He stared wide eyed across the room at her. Atop the desk, crouching over him, stood a black-eyed devil, arms crimson from where they delved into Liam's open chest. It was from this cavity that the wet sucking noises emanated. Despite having the organs removed and arranged about the desk, it seemed her son was still alive.

As she stepped over the threshold, she felt the weight of the devil's black eyes upon her. It hopped off her son and stood ramrod straight, facing her. It grinned at her like the Cheshire Cat and, with great deliberateness, it licked the blood from its fingers one by one, savoring it. Catherine thought her eyes played tricks on her; the fingers were impossibly long and moved more like tentacles than human digits.

Behind the devil, a last tear fell from her son's eye as he gave up the ghost. She saw the life fade from him and felt an emptiness in the room, echoed by the hollow within. "Liam..." she whispered.

The devil took this as its queue. It strode up to her and snaked fingers around her face. "It's been too long, Catherine. Now, where is that darling girl?"

Black despair descended upon Catherine. She knew

what she had to do. She brought the straight razor up and cut a deep slit into her own throat. It hurt. *God, does it hurt!* But she forced herself to bring the blade across her neck, for Rose's sake. As her vision darkened beneath the fear of the eternal black that waited for her, she felt something snake-like slide into the severed blood vessels and slip inside her brain. Then nothing else remained.

CHAPTER 6

THE HOUND

Fiachra MacTire sat hunched over on the functional cell bunk like a desiccated gargoyle. He reflected upon his sorry state of confinement and was in a morose mood because if it. This was bad for one of his kind, but expected given the circumstances. They had confined him to his current lodgings for over a decade, after all.

Apart from the bunk upon which he sat, the cell held only rudimentary furnishings: a rough-hewn table and accompanying chair, a cracked basin for washing, a bucket to piss and shit in, and a shelf to hold his worldly possessions. His worldly possessions comprised basic toiletries, eating utensils, and a battered Bible. He'd ram the last item down the throat of the Sister who left him that.

How he had raged when they'd first put him there. He was a descendent of the Kings of Ossory. How dare they keep him captive like a lowly mongrel? He had tried to transform into wolf form, but they had somehow curtailed his power. His fragile, human form had paid the price for his anger. They later informed him of the silver strands woven within the walls and door. They held him good. *A*

42

plague on you, Sisters, he thought, for the hundred-thousandth time.

He had forced their hand eventually, of course. They had dropped their guard once, before the silver, and seeing an opportunity, he'd escaped their clutches. He'd made it to the docks and stowed away, making it as far as the new world. What times he had experienced there. He chuckled, a sad dry thing that echoed in the cell. *Such freedom.* A wry smile danced on his lips, but it vanished rapidly.

Six Sisters had caught up with him in a small desert town in New Mexico. Those hellish witches caught him with his guard down; he'd been full sure they'd never find him, much less follow him there. He'd underestimated their persistence. *I won't do so again.* Now all that remained of that time were the memories. And maybe, if he checked the cell's floor, a few grains of New Mexico sand.

Upon returning to his confinement after his brief raging, he'd settled onto the crude bed provided and awaited whatever fate would befall. He'd slept for a year, here and there.

The cell was bland and far from stimulating. He'd counted the cracks in the floor, ceiling, and walls too many times to remember. Most recently, he'd distracted himself by studying a scrawny spider in the corner above the door as it watched its web; both Fiachra and spider awaited a fly. He called the spider The Mother after his captor, but alas, there were no flies in the cell but him.

The preceding morning had been different. As he watched The Mother sitting patiently on her web, he sensed disruption in the world above. *A change is in the air,* he thought. He'd been sitting on the edge of his bed ever since, as though he was the spider, spinning a web to catch whatever prey approached.

~

It was hours later, and Fiachra paced. The cell was only three strides, but he paced. His face inches from the wall, he about turned and paced.

One, two, three, turn...

His skin burned as the surrounding poisonous metal thwarted his body's desire to transform. Staying still was unbearable; the cell's walls closed in on him. So he paced.

One, two, three, turn...

He couldn't grasp how the witches dared to confine him so. What right had they? From what he had seen of them, they were more demon than he. *Unnatural things!* He stopped in the centre of the cell and threw his head up to where the moon would be. His mournful howl echoed from the walls, but none of his brethren were near. And so Fiachra paced again.

One, two, thr-

He stopped mid-stride, having heard the aged hinges creak in the tunnels beyond the cell. He turned to face the door. With head cocked, he listened. There were no footsteps, but he heard the shift of cloth on cloth and the unmistakable sound of an elongated, dying gasp. *The witches.*

As the key rattled the lock to his cell door, Fiachra prepared to spring.

The door swung inwards, and the Sister entered. She held aloft a Celtic wolf knot, a symbol of his kind, but wrought in silver. He stepped back from it and composed himself as befit his station, while inwardly he raged at their insult. "Good morning, witch," he said, in a growling voice, almost unfamiliar to him from the lack of use.

"There is a task for you, hound," she said.

The epithet grated, but he let it slide. He started it; he supposed. "Of course, Sister. I live but to serve." The flourish was a mockery, but the Sister passed no regard that he could see. *Those damned masks,* he thought.

"You will locate an item for The Mother and return it to her," the Sister instructed.

"And why would I do that?" he asked, as pleasantly as he could manage.

"If you complete this task, The Mother will have no further need for you. If you return the item, along with the thief who has it, we will release you."

Fiachra mulled over the offer, as if he had a better one. He was no fool and knew he couldn't trust the witches. But if agreement freed him from this place of confinement, he didn't care about the terms. "I'll do it," he said.

The Sister nodded, pleased at his lip-service, and stepped backwards out of the cell. Two more sisters entered, one brandishing metalworking tools, the other a thick silver bracelet.

Fiachra stepped back from the poisonous metal instinctively, but there was nowhere to go. He was too weak to fight them, and he could see what they wanted, so he held out his left arm and gritted his teeth.

The Sisters made quick work of attaching the silver band to his forearm and stepped backwards from him and out of the cell once done.

Fiachra's skin burned where it came in contact with the silver band, and if there was any food in his stomach, he was sure he'd have left it on the cell floor. The first Sister came to the doorway again, and he said, "There was no need for that."

The Sister ignored his comment and moved away. "This way, hound."

He stepped after her and then past her when she instructed, "Straight on." It grated on him that his obedience was a given. Grated even more that he had no other option but to obey. *For now.* He moved down the dank tunnel in the direction dictated, noting the sound of cloth against cloth as the Sister fell in behind him. He was glad she couldn't see the menace in his eyes.

Despite the hobbling silver band, for the first time in over a decade, Fiachra was excited. He had plans. He would do as bidden, of course, but he would do it in his own time. Feeding was foremost on his mind. He would satisfy his hunger first. And when he saw a chance to escape from them for good, he would take it. *Then I'll destroy these witches once and for all.*

Before Fiachra knew it, he was on the street. He revelled in the sights and sounds of Dublin. In the past, he had hated concentrated humanity, and the noise and filth that often accompanied them, but a decade of confinement had mellowed him, it seemed. *All this meat!*

He had left the dungeon through a passageway that led to a cellar beneath a temple of the Christ god. No priest attended at that late hour and the Sister had ushered him down the aisle and out the front door. "Go. And be quick about it, hound." Without waiting for a reply, she slammed the temple door.

And as suddenly as that, he found himself left to his own devices, at least for a time. He sauntered down the stone steps to the street, conscious of his weakened state.

"Jaysus, would ya look at this fella?" A scruffy old-timer,

in a suit which had seen better days, stood gaping at him from the footpath.

Fiachra looked down at his body and noticed for the first time that he wore but a pair of breeches. His body was severely malnourished, having subsisted on a diet of meagre rations from the Sisters and whatever insects or vermin he could catch. The silver still seared his arm and there was a faint odour of burning hair and flesh. But, even hampered by the toxic metal, he felt his snout distend somewhat and noticed his pelt grew in, if somewhat patchy. His condition fostered many strange looks from the passing nighttime crowd.

He saluted the old timer, said "Good night to you," in a growl, and loped away from the temple steps.

The Sisters had made a colossal mistake, though they did not yet know it. They had released him from his bonds to locate their trinket. But he had no desire to return to imprisonment. He would find the staff they sought, and the man who held it, but he would be their captive no more. *I will find it and be done with them!*

Fiachra checked each side street and alleyway he passed until he found a suitably isolated one, out of sight of passersby. He closed his eyes and reached for his wolf-form beneath his man-shape. Sweat beaded his brow as he pushed through the pain caused by the silver shackle. Slowly, and with great effort, his wolf-form came through: snout elongated, a patchwork of fur appeared, emaciated muscles grew less emaciated. It was far from a complete transformation, not even close to his full strength, but even so, he luxuriated in the vastly superior sense of smell. His knees almost gave way; he could truly see the world again. *How can humans survive their blindness?*

Fiachra inhaled deeply, building a scent map of his

surrounds. Food abounded all around. He crept to the mouth of the alley and waited. Before long, a lone man sauntered by, whistling to himself. From the scent of alcohol wafting Fiachra's way, the man had had a few. All the better until he regained his strength.

Fiachra waited until the drunkard passed before launching at the man's exposed neck. He crushed the spine with a savage bite that dropped the man before he could react. The man's eyes were wide as Fiachra dragged him into the alley.

Cloaked in shadows, Fiachra tore into the man's abdomen while the man looked on. He whimpered as Fiachra consumed his organs one by one. When the lungs filled with blood, the man's whimpers became gurgles until the blood spilled from his mouth and nostrils. Fiachra consumed the still beating heart last, and the man finally passed.

Fiachra found the wall of the alley and lay back against it, satiated. It had been too long since he'd had proper food; the witches only gave him enough to keep him alive, and then barely. The drunkard's inebriated state also gave him a yearning for spirits; he could taste the alcohol in the man's flesh and blood. He already felt his body repair itself, but the silver hampered the process. *I'll get rid of the damned thing yet!* He grabbed the silver band in his right hand, intending to wrench it from his left forearm, but as soon as his fingers touched the metal, he had to pull them back. It was worse than being scorched by fire, compounding the pain of where the silver came into contact with his arm.

After a minute's rest, in which he got his laboured breath under control again, he looked around the alley. He spotted a puddle of ground water and moved to it to clean up as best he could. Then he pulled the coat from the man's body and threw it around his shoulders. *Pity I ruined the shirt,* he thought. He'd be more careful the next time. Next, he would find a dangerous place to drink worse liquor and to Hell with the Sisters. He slipped back into his man-shape and strolled from the alley. *But first let me see if someone else can relieve me of this silver.*

WITH LITTLE EFFORT, Fiachra had picked up a tail. He'd found a suitably downscale síbín and affected a drunken demeanour whilst flashing the silver on his arm for all to see. He'd heard careful footfalls behind him as he staggered away. Footfalls that kept pace with him as he walked unsteadily along the street, never too close but also never far back. He stepped into a doorway and leaned against the wall to relieve himself. As the piss flowed, he heard the footfalls stop, then an indecisive scuffle of boots, followed by their fast approach.

He maintained his mummery as a heavy hand fell on his shoulder and turned him about. He doused his assailant's trouser legs with his pungent, dehydrated piss.

"What the hell!?" said an unfortunate face, made worse by a twist of disgust. The grip on Fiachra was unwavering, though.

"Beg your pardon, good sir," said Fiachra with a slurred voice.

"I'll show you pardon, you cursed foozler," said the man as he pulled Fiachra from the doorway and dragged him into a side street. The man administered a brutal stomach punch which knocked the wind out of Fiachra and sent him to the floor. "I'll be having that bracelet, if you don't mind."

Curled up on the detritus strewn cobbles, and in

genuine pain, Fiachra fought to reign in his anger. As much as he wanted to tear the man apart, he wanted rid of the silver band more.

The man kneeled on Fiachra's upper left arm to secure it, then pulled the arm up to examine the band. He made a low *whistle*. "That's pure silver, I'd swear to it," he said, twisting Fiachra's arm about to view every side. "Where's the clasp?"

When Fiachra didn't respond, the man wrenched his arm to an impossible position, causing Fiachra to cry out in pain. The arm was on the cusp of breaking, Fiachra was sure, but he saw no mercy in that cruel face, so he didn't respond.

Getting no answer, the man set to pulling the band up the arm, towards the wrist and hand. With each inch, the fresh contact seared Fiachra's flesh, and he gritted his teeth in pain. The man sniffed. "What's that smell?" He brought his nose to the band. "Smells like bacon. What the fuck is this?" But he kept pulling the band until it reached Fiachra's hand.

Fiachra was close to passing out, but he fought to hold on. *Must. See. This. Through.*

The man strained for what seemed like an eternity, trying to pull the band over his hand, before giving up with a "Whoreson!" He drew a filthy-looking blade from his belt. "Guess you won't be needing that thumb." He sliced into the flesh between Fiachra's index finger and thumb.

With a *roar*, the beast broke through. Fiachra's right hand shot up, taking hold of the man's coat collar, and throwing him towards the nearby wall. The man hit hard, twisting his knife-hand awkwardly. The wrist snapped with a sharp *crack* and the man cried out as he dropped to the ground.

Fiachra was on the man's back before he could rise. Gripping his head in both hands, he smashed his face into the ground. The man's nose broke and his teeth splintered as Fiachra repeatedly brought his face down upon the cobbles. Soon there was no face to speak of, only a concave bloody mess in its place.

When the man showed no more signs of life, Fiachra calmed and stepped back to survey his work. The man's legs kicked spasmodically, but Fiachra was sure the man wouldn't rise. *Not with that face,* he thought. Fiachra was pleased to note that the man's clothing was relatively untouched by the gore.

He dragged the body deeper into the darkness and made quick work of stripping it, but did not don the clothing just yet. Retrieving the filthy knife, Fiachra cut the skin of the man's chest and pealed it back to reveal the breastbone and ribcage. He lined up the tip of the knife with the centre of the breastbone and struck the hilt with his palm to crack the bone. Then he pulled open the ribcage like two sides of a flesh crab carapace.

Fiachra salivated at the glistening organs inside. He set to work devouring them one by one, feeling his body respond to the meat instantly. When he could eat no more, he lay back on the ground next to the leftovers. He let out a loud *burp*. "Pardon me."

After allowing his meal to digest, he stood up, feeling renewed. The silver still burned, but his returned strength made it more bearable. He wiped the blood and gore from his latest meal on the jacket he'd picked up earlier from his first meal. He then dressed in his new clothing. They were a loose fit on his still emaciated form, but he'd work on that. With a spring in his step, he left the sidestreet in search of the nearest síbín.

CHAPTER 7
REUNION

He is a boy again, uncertain of his age, but, like most arriving in Dublin, fleeing the horror of the countryside, he is old beyond mere years.

He and what remains of his family come as a last resort, but find that the only difference the city makes is that there's no peaceful place to die. Death always has an audience, for the poor anyway.

They were not poor anymore, though. Father had seen to that. Upon reaching Dublin, they had enough money to live the life of the rich. But at what cost?

His father is changed, different from the man he was before the famine years. Darker. More distant. When had he last heard his father's laughter? But if not for the sacrifices made, they wouldn't have survived the last years in the countryside. Not him, nor any of them. For that, he would always be grateful, but he mourned the loss of the father he remembered.

He moves forward in time, just a few years. He is still in school. It's break time, and he is in the yard, surrounded by a group of boys. They push him and pull him every which way, call him names, spit on him - they know there's something different about him, but even amongst themselves they cannot tell what that difference is.

The trouble escalates, and the children throw punches and kicks. He falls to the ground and curls up in a ball to protect himself. As he slips into unconsciousness, he hears the bell announcing the end of lunch break.

He is pushed forward in time again, or maybe he is drawn, he can't tell, and the ringing changes its tone to become the gentle ringing of a bicycle bell. He's in St Stephen's Green in the heart of Dublin. It's a summer's day, one he could never forget. It's the first time he saw Nemhain. On this day, his life changed, and he finally saw a way out of the darkness which had ever overshadowed his life. The vision on the bicycle was apologising to him as he lay on the ground, having just been knocked over by her. On a tree branch, behind Nemhain, a large crow watched their meeting with interest.

LORCAN SURFACED FROM HIS DREAM, a smile still faint upon his lips. He reached across the bed. "Nemhain," he said. He grasped at the fading dream, tried to pull it to him, but the emptiness shocked him awake. He was sure in that moment, on the cusp of consciousness, that he would touch her soft warmth. The faint odour of her perfume was in the air, he was sure of it. He'd suffered such nightmares over the past two decades and was always relieved to elude them; the wonderful dreams made the waking world a nightmare. His past happiness haunted him. *What time is it?*

However long he had slept, he didn't feel rested. He was in bed, but he had no recollection of getting there, or indeed where the bed was. Church bells tolled outside the window. *The sheep summoned to Mass, perhaps?* He couldn't comprehend how people could worship the intangible without questioning. His only faith was rooted in his family. He had worshipped his wife and son. *See how that ended,* he thought, the bitterness catching him by surprise.

Lorcan saw nothing to gain by remaining in bed. He had much to do. Throwing off the sheets, he hopped onto the chilly morning floor. He felt good, better than he'd felt in years. The familiar morning aches and pains were absent, and he felt strong. He clenched his fists, luxuriating in his own strength.

Then he noticed the blood. It flaked at the touch; blood from hands to elbow and no wound in sight. He surmised it belonged to someone else until the night's deeds came back to him and a wave of dizziness dropped him to his knees. *What have I done?* He realised where he was then; the room he and Nemhain had shared during their marriage. He must have come there after he had... finished downstairs.

He looked at the bed and saw sheets caked with more dried blood. Then he spotted his reflection in the half-length mirror standing in the room's corner. His clothing was a bloody mess.

He caught sight of the staff laying on the floor next to the bed. He picked it up and flung it across the room, where it crashed against the wall with a satisfying thump. It didn't break, more's the pity. *Cursed thing!*

Making no effort to clean himself, Lorcan investigated the rest of the house to confirm that his memories weren't a nightmare. The three bodies lay where he'd left them, defiled and open to the world. The man servant in the hall, the new master of the house, and his old housekeeper, Catherine, in the study. All three were spoiling, but he covered them as best he could. He could offer little else.

Lorcan remembered the young girl then. *Rose.* Thankfully, she was nowhere to be seen. He didn't want the blood of children on his hands. *I'll leave this world without that, at least.* The carnage in the house made him more resolute than ever to do what he'd come back to the city to do. He was determined to join Nemhain and Cormac that very day, before whatever malady had taken him the previous night struck him again.

Back in the bedroom, he raided the dresser and wardrobe for something less gory to wear. The master was almost of a size with him and he found a smart suit which he lay to one side. He also found the master's shaving equipment, but the razor was missing. A flash of Catherine cutting her throat hit him and he winced. He returned to her body to retrieve the blade, breaking her fingers to free it before cleaning it of her blood.

From the kitchen, he fetched a kettle of boiling water. He stripped and washed the worst of the blood off first, then half-filled the basin with hot water, unrolled the shaving kit, and prepared his face for grooming; a month's worth of growth had to be dealt with. The blade's familiar shape was a comfort in his hand. A quality cut-throat razor always stirred Lorcan's blood. He had a penchant for knives - they pleased him more than a firearm ever could - but a cut-throat razor was a thing of beauty. Light as a feather, lethal in a practiced hand and unnoticeable when slipped into a boot or up a sleeve. He felt no guilt at using the blade for its intended purpose, despite its recent grim history.

He felt better after the shave, like a civilised human being again. He was not averse to facial hair, had often worn beards of various styles to fit fashion or his mood. Nemhain had preferred him clean-shaven, so he'd be that way when he met her in the next world.

Next, he dressed in a suit, shirt, and tie. The pressed

clothing felt good on his skin, and he admired the cut of himself in the mirror. He felt as though something was missing, but a scan of the room revealed his sheathed kukri lying on the ground. It appeared that he hadn't used it, as he couldn't remember taking it off the night before and it was still clean. He stared at it for a full minute in silent debate with himself over whether he should bring it along. *Better have it than regret not having it,* he thought and scooped it up. He removed his jacket again to strap it on and felt immediately better by its presence at his back.

Donning the jacket, he left his bedroom and made for the kitchen. He needed to eat before venturing out. *What's a fitting last meal?* Something simple. He prepared thick slices of buttered bread, cheese, and ham, all washed down with cool water. He had been famished. After eating, he prepared a cup of tea, sweetened it, and drank it down as he went over his plan. *Find the place they died and pay my respects. Once that is done...* He shied away from what would come after. *Best not to dwell on it.*

Leaving what remained of his meal on the table, Lorcan went to the entrance hall. He donned his stolen coat and closed the townhouse door behind him for what he was sure would be the last time. He set off towards Sackville Street.

FEA MURRIGAN AWOKE TO SUFFERING. She'd cracked her head on something solid and, wincing, opened her eyes to slits. She lay on the floor of a compact compartment which jostled her back and forth. Dim light entered through a crack in the drawn curtain above, but only half-heartedly made it to her. *A Carriage?* Judging by the vibrations, it ran over uneven ground. Attempting to rise, pain lanced through her body. Her hands were bound in front with a coarse rope. She also felt groggy. *What had happened?*

Casting her mind back, Fea remembered holing up in an abandoned shack close to Kingstown Harbor. She and two other runaways waited on a man who would bring them to a paddle-ship steamer destined for Holyhead across the Irish Sea. It had taken her a hard week of travelling by stars and moonlight to get there, and she could almost taste the freedom of English shores. But something had gone wrong. *A pox on Karl Murphy!*

She'd met the man, the boy she corrected herself, for he was of an age with her, on the morning of her approach to Kingstown village. The sky lightened with the coming of dawn and she was desperate to find somewhere to hide out for the day. Her thoughts were full of what she'd do once she was finally free. By the time she saw Karl, it was too late.

"Pleasant morning for a walk," he'd said.

She hadn't wanted to make conversation with him, but he had an amiable smile and a gentle way about him, and he was persistent. It had been so long since she had spoken to anyone and before long, he seemed like an old friend. *Stupid girl!*

With a supreme effort, fuelled by her anger at herself, Fea struggled first to her knees and then onto the carriage seat, keeping her balance despite the carriage's motion. A wave of nausea came over her and she almost heaved. She fought it down.

She had thought herself so clever to turn the conversation to the nearby port. A casual expression of her desire to make passage to England and Karl had jumped at the chance to help her. It was no big deal to arrange a discreet passage, he'd told her, for his uncle knew a man who could be trusted, for a modest price. *Modest price? Pah! For Who?*

A pounding ache began somewhere deep inside her head.

She'd given Karl what money she had, money lifted from those bitches of nuns she'd escaped from, and later that day he'd brought her to the rickety shed. Crammed into it with two other poor unfortunates, she felt like a cow, or a pig, or some other helpless, stupid creature. When Karl arrived at the appointed time, he was not alone. Three other burly men were with him. Fea knew by the hungry look in their eyes that there was going to be trouble. She also knew that she would cause them more trouble than they'd bargained for.

She shuddered at the memory, but it was lost in the carriage's uneven gait. Lifting her bound hands to her face, she saw fingernails clogged with dried blood. She dropped them to her lap, taking in the torn and filthy state of her dress - much worse a toll than her journey had taken. She shifted in the seat to move closer to the carriage window, grunting at the pain coming from her battered body. A sharp pain pulsed from her womanhood, and it brought tears to her eyes, but she shook them away. *Time for crying later.*

She pulled the curtain open to reveal a city scene. As the carriage crossed a wide bridge, a well-dressed man standing on the wall at the bridge's edge captured Fea's attention. *Jesus, he's going to jump!* Her woes forgotten, she battered her bloodied hands against the carriage window.

THE WIND WHIPPED Lorcan's coat around his legs, ushering him to the edge of the wall. Despite its chill, the wind possessed a seductive quality. The water below was dark and menacing in the morning light, chopped by the rain and easterly gusts. He wondered how many times he'd thought of giving himself to this river over the past score of years. How many times had he imagined sinking below the murky surface and breathing her water into his lungs? He shuddered—not a pleasant thought. If not for his wife and son walking this path before him, he would never choose this as his end. He had always hated the water, even as a child.

"Yer not goin' to jump in, are ye?"

Lorcan turned towards this question and saw a diminutive gentleman with a peaked cap perched on his head, looking up at him with interest. "And what if I am?"

The man shrugged. "Nothin' to me, really."

Lorcan turned back, prepared himself.

"Looks frigid in there this morning, though."

Lorcan ignored the little man.

"Not that you'll notice in a bit, eh?"

Lorcan took a deep breath. "What?" he asked.

"You won't notice the cold soon. Since you'll be dead an' all."

Lorcan turned to face the man again. "Do you mind? This isn't as easy as it looks," he explained.

"Fair enough."

Lorcan turned and prepared once more.

"It's just that, since you won't be needin' it an' all. Can I have your coat?"

Lorcan was incredulous. "Fuck off," he said.

"Ohhhh. Sorry I spoke." The man had the cheek to look offended as he continued across the bridge.

Lorcan watched him stroll away for a moment, then turned back to his task. He inhaled a deep breath in preparation. The time had come. *I'll see you soon, Nemhain.* As he shut his eyes, he heard a loud banging from the street behind him. Glancing over his shoulder, he located the source - a passing carriage. A girl banged on the glass window, making an awful racket. It's a wonder the glass held up to it. Lorcan squinted; there was something familiar about her. And then it struck him like a physical blow. "Nemhain?"

A forceful blast of wind hit him, and he lost his footing. He almost toppled into the dark bitch of a river before regaining his balance. *Get down, you fool, before you kill yourself.* He hopped off the wall and stood on the footpath, watching the carriage as it made the north side of the bridge and turned right off Sackville Street. *Strange,* he thought. Seeing a black shape, keep pace with the carriage and turn where it turned. *Is that a crow?*

As to the carriage's occupant, Lorcan knew it couldn't be Nemhain. The girl was twenty years too young for a start. But for her to appear before him at that moment couldn't be a coincidence. Lorcan didn't believe in coincidences. He set off after the receding carriage and the shade of his long-dead wife.

CHAPTER 8
FEA

Fiachra's head pounded from the aftereffects of the copious amount of alcohol he'd consumed over the preceding hours. *Never again!* From now on, he'd avoid drunken prey to break a fast. It was far too easy to lose his inhibitions and yearn for more, and he didn't want to end up in such a sorry state again.

With much effort, he found the last known location of the object he sought. The Sister's directions had got him most of the way and his enhanced senses allowed him to home in on the area of recent slaughter. The stench of magic and spilled blood still permeated the air.

A light fog swirled around his feet as he studied what tracks remained in the ash pit. He smelled the acrid, corrupt scent of magic as an upper layer, and the unmistakable scent of the witches as a recent addition. The potent smell of blood was there too, making him salivate, but beneath that lay the hint of three humans, two young ones and an older male. The young ones went in one direction, the man in the opposite. "Which of you have the damned staff?" he asked aloud, then winced at the pain in the temple his own voice caused.

"Who are ye talkin' to, sor?" A woman emerged from the fog, ragged and filthy. Scents of sweat and disease fought for dominance. She moved close to him and thrust her sex at him. She rubbed suggestively but mechanically, a well-practiced motion. "Are ye lookin' for a good time?" she asked him, attempting a seductive purr.

She was drunk, or perhaps narcotics hazed her mind, because she didn't react as his face changed into wolf-form. By the time realisation dawned in her eyes, he had lunged at her and ripped out her throat's ability to scream. He ate in peace, undisturbed by her, devouring the parts that weren't wholly rotted through.

Once done, a modicum of strength returned, and the pain at his temples subsided. He felt better, but far from fully recovered from his overindulgence. She hadn't been drunk and the narcotics she was on had minimal effect on his system. He was grateful for that because he had work to do.

Bringing his attention back to the task at hand, he considered the two sets of tracks; the two youngsters or the adult, which to pursue? His mouth watered at the thoughts of tender young prey. *The young ones*, he decided, unashamedly led by his stomach.

He stripped the shawl from the gory mess at his feet and wiped his face and hands before throwing it back on the whore. Then, hunched over, he half ran, half loped through the labyrinth of alleyways following the faint trail left by what he imagined were most succulent prey.

❧

I can't believe I ran away into this. Fea stood in the opulent room they had brought her to following the carriage journey. She shivered uncontrollably and tensing to stop it, just increased its violence. Her body couldn't take much more. The scrutiny of the woman standing in the doorway didn't help matters. Fea felt like a prize pig being led to the market. *Or a lamb to slaughter.*

The woman entered the room with an elegant step. As she approached, Fea noticed her dark clothing was of the finest quality. "You are in a state, aren't you?" the woman said in an accent Fea thought might be French. The woman *tut-tutted* as she stopped before Fea and scrutinised her. "You're a pretty one and spirited, but keep in mind that in my Flash House there's a fine line between spirited and more trouble than you're worth." The woman reached out and grabbed Fea's face. She squeezed her cheeks together, digging her thumb and fingers hard into the flesh. "Girls who are more trouble than they are worth in my brothel end up in Westmoreland Lock Hospital, and treatment there for trouble is smotheration. Some are even sent to Gloucester Street Laundry and wish they'd been sent to the Hospital instead." She let Fea go with a look of disgust and returned to the doorway.

Jesus wept! I'm in a brothel? Fea had thought that she had hit her lowest point, but as the realisation of her current situation sank in, she felt as though a trapdoor had opened beneath her and she had dropped through. She had yet to reach the ground. Something hardened within her at that moment, and she knew she would not suffer another man laying a forceful hand on her. *I'll murder him or die trying.*

The madam was watching her, and Fea hoped she had not betrayed her intent somehow.

"You will be ready for tonight. We are short one girl and we will need you. I trust there'll be no nonsense from you?"

"No, miss," said Fea.

"Good," Madam Arnott said in satisfaction before leaving.

A matronly woman holding a basin and cloth bustled into the room. Kneeling before Fea, the woman looked her over. "You shouldn't have struggled, girl. It only encourages them." She smiled as she spoke, to take any bite from the words. "Let's get you cleaned up, eh?"

The woman's touch was gentle, to match her voice, and the hot water felt good on Fea's skin. Over the next hour, as the woman tended to her, Fea fell into a daze. The woman bathed her, plucked her, preened her, and powdered her. She applied a lightening agent to Fea's complexion and added rouge to enliven it. She then dressed Fea in clothing to suit her figure, both under clothing and that which would cover it, however temporary that might be. It was an ordeal for Fea. She hated dressing up. On the exterior, though, she appeared compliant, while within, she plotted and planned.

TOMMY WOKE with a start and looked around the room with the confused gaze of one fresh from dreaming. Something was amiss, but it took a moment for him to identify it. The morning was unusually bright for this time. Tommy's eyes widened, and he jumped up, causing Margaret to fall over and start awake too. "Shite!" he said.

"What's wrong, Tommy? Is he here?" she asked, jumping to her feet.

"I'm feckin' late!" he said, panic entering his voice. *The madam will kill me!* He scanned the room for the other kids, but they didn't seem to pay him any mind, so he pulled the previous night's takings and covertly handed them to his sister. Taking the bundle, she looked at it with a dumbfounded expression. "Put it away before someone sees it!" he hissed.

Margaret secreted them in her frayed cardigan.

"We'll see what the pawnbroker will give for them after my shift, okay?"

Margaret nodded.

"Are you okay?" he asked her.

"What do you mean?"

"Last night..." he began, then searched for the right words. "That thing..."

"I'm okay," she said in a muted voice he wasn't sure he liked.

"Just stay here, around people. I'll be back tonight." Leaving his sister standing in the mouldering room with silent tears rolling down her grimy face, Tommy navigated around the pathetic forms of destitute children on his way to the door. He looked back, feeling guilty and helpless to do anything about it. Even if they could afford for him to miss the shift at the flash house, he'd feel the full wrath of Madam Arnott once he surfaced again. "Please, God. Look after her while I'm away," he whispered as he left the room, unaware that one form he passed had been watching them attentively.

LORCAN LOITERED in a doorway across the street from the house where the carriage halted, and where they had taken his dead wife's doppelgänger. He knew it was a flash house, as he had observed the constant activity of its patrons all morning. The only grace in the woman being taken to this building rather than one further down the street was that it looked to be a high-end house. *Less chance of disease,* he thought with a grimace.

Lorcan had been out of breath from keeping pace with the carriage as it travelled from the bridge on Lower Sackville Street, along Eden Quay as far as the Custom House, and then to Mecklenburg via Store Street and Mabbot Street. He'd lost sight of the carriage frequently, but always found it again by following its trailing crow. He looked up and spotted the creature sitting on the edge of the roof three stories up. Lorcan had the uncomfortable sensation that it watched him as he watched the house.

When the carriage turned into Monto, Lorcan's heart sank. *This doesn't bode well,* he'd thought. The house he now watched confirmed his earlier feeling. *I can walk away. She's nothing to me.* But as soon as it occurred to him, he dismissed it. The girl could be Nemhain's twin; to see her at the moment he would end his life, to join Nemhain and Cormac, was too strange a coincidence for Lorcan to dismiss. The circumstances forced him to find out if the girl was alright, and if she wasn't, he'd lend what aid he could. Nemhain's shade compelled him to, or at least his remembrance of her did.

Lorcan was no stranger to the Monto area. He had frequented its síbíns and flash-houses regularly in the wild days of his youth. The sights and sounds of the busy street brought back those days of wandering in search of adventure, but invariably finding nothing but trouble. The previous evening, he found himself drawn to the area, craving the sights and sounds of those days.

He moved out of his vantage point and bought a penny

pie from a nearby street vendor, still blending in as much as possible as he planned. Biting into the pastry filled his mouth with the warm gravy. He polished off the rest without dwelling on the meat inside - he was sure he had eaten worse. When he finished, he bought a half mug of coffee from a stall further down Mecklenburg Street. Gulping the hot, strong liquid down, he felt ready for what lay ahead.

The street was becoming thronged. Far greater numbers of uniforms roamed here than he remembered, predominantly soldiers from Aldborough Barracks a few streets away, he supposed. The docks were close too, adding sailors to the mix. All sought relief from a life lived with other men; many would return home with more than they bargained for: pissing pins and needles, a shanker, or worse. He shivered at the thought, having experienced venereal disease first-hand over the years of his travels.

All things considered, the men had the better deal. Life was fraught with danger for the women who sold themselves there. If a beating or a knife didn't swiftly see them to their grave, one disease or another definitely would. *You don't see many old whores.* Lorcan thought again of his wife's simulacrum in the house across the street and his stomach flipped. He knew he had to get moving and his first order of business was to get inside that house.

He caught sight of a short figure weaving rapidly through the passersby and recognised it as the lad from the previous night. *Where are you rushing to?* Careful to remain out of sight, it surprised Lorcan when the lad charged up the steps to the very door he watched. A succession of small raps and the door opened a crack before the brutal-looking doorman allowed him entrance without a word. *Interesting,* thought Lorcan, but he felt a chill as another seeming coincidence fell into place.

For him, it was the final decider; he couldn't help but think something guided him to that place and he had no choice but to act. "Fate loves the fearless," he said, and before he could think any more about it, he walked over and rap-rapped confidently on the door, glad he'd cleaned himself up that morning.

MARGARET HUNKERED in the spot where she and Tommy had spent the night, shivering now that her brother's warmth was absent. The bundle, concealed in her top, possessed a weight that exceeded its physicality, and she longed for a hiding place to keep it until a later time. But she didn't want to move because Tommy told her not to.

Across the small room, one bundle of clothing moved and stood to a height taller than a child. The gaunt face of Ratso Kelly turned her way, and he gazed at her for a moment before turning away. That gaze put the fear of God into Margaret.

Ratso traversed the room, stepping over bundled children with his gangling legs, stopping and crouching and whispering in two places before moving to the door. Two more bundles expanded and walked to where Ratso waited.

Margaret couldn't tear her eyes away from the trio, who whispered and stole glances at her. She had a bad, dropping sensation in her stomach.

After a minute of conversation, Ratso and the other two stood. One of the two closed the door, and all three crossed the room like a pack of weasels fresh out of a ditch. Ratso took the middle, the others the sides. Margaret felt like a little frog, but she didn't dare hop away from them for fear of what they'd do.

The three soon loomed over her. "Give us what you 'ave," said Ratso, in a nasal whine. His wedge-shaped face caused unusually large front teeth to jut in her direction. She might have laughed, had Tommy been there cracking jokes, and they were a safe distance away, but there was nothing funny about the meanness in the older boy's eyes.

"I... d-d-don't have nothing, Ratso," she said. As soon as she uttered his nickname, she knew she'd made a mistake.

Ratso's countenance darkened. "What did you say?" he whine-whispered as he lowered his face to hers.

Tears sprang from Margaret's eyes, but she wiped them quickly away.

One accomplice snickered while the other one said, "Aw, the likkle baby's cryin'."

Trying to be brave like she knew Tommy would be, Margaret dug her fingernails into the palms of her hands and stood up straight. "I don't have nothing," she said, looking Ratso in the eyes.

"Hmm," he said and moved his head back. Then, quick as a snake, his knobby fist swung in and crashed into her stomach.

The breath whooshed out of Margaret and her eyes widened as the unexpected pain took her.

As the diminutive girl slumped to the floor, Ratso stood to his full height, a satisfied smile on his thin lips. "Search the little bitch," he ordered his snickering companion.

His accomplice bent over Margaret, who still fought to catch her breath, and after a quick search, came back up with the bundle of takings.

Ratso held out his hand, and he gave the bundle over.

Ratso nodded approvingly at the weight of it, then stepped in and kicked Margaret in the ribs.

She couldn't cry out in pain because her breath wasn't back yet, but the agony she felt was evident in her expression.

"Next time I tell ya to give me somethin' just do it," he said.

The trio turned away from where she lay helpless and found a quiet spot against the opposite wall. They hunkered around to count their takings.

Margaret finally drew a ragged breath and winced in pain. She moved on all fours to her secluded space and silently prayed for Tommy's swift return.

FEA MOVED from room to room, careful not to dally too long in any one area. She figured that if she kept constantly moving between rooms and floors, she might buy herself enough time to escape before she had to tumble a so-called 'gentleman'. Failing that, if she got cornered, she would work on getting her suitor too drunk to perform between the sheets. If both tactics failed, she didn't know what she'd do precisely, but it would require a weapon of some sort. She'd been keeping an eye out for something suitable since she'd left the room she'd dressed in. *I'll kill them before I let them touch me,* she swore to herself. The words were iron, propping her up where she might have crumpled without them.

Her virginity or lack of experience wasn't the issue - she had previous suitors and had equally relished their company. However, the idea of prostituting herself to a fool for money, of being commodified with no control over the buyer, disgusted her. An image of Karl Murphy leering down at her as two brutes held her down flashed before her eyes, but she pushed it back down to where she'd buried it. The memory was powerful enough to bring her to an abrupt stop, and it took a monumental effort to smother it back down. *I can't deal with that now!* The moment passed, and she unclenched her fists and breathed again.

For the past hour, she had laughed at the jokes of patrons and danced with them, pretending to drink every drink that was given. She was not sure how much liquor the poor houseplants would take before they withered up and died. *Giving up all my secrets.*

"You are a pretty little thing." The dandy materialised from out of nowhere, all hands and leering eyes. Without ceremony, he had a hand up her skirt, between her legs. "I'll have a tumble with you, I think."

When the shock of this assault on her senses, this successful breach, had worn off, Fea's reply was swift. She stood on the fool's foot and moved in close. The sudden speed made him attempt a retreat, but the trapped foot only landed him on the floor in an undignified heap with his drink adorning his suit. "I'm terribly sorry, sir. Let me fetch a cloth to clean you up." She turned on her tail and began the process of evasion once more.

"Well played, miss," said a gruff voice from behind her.

She abruptly turned towards the man who addressed her, worried at how much he'd seen.

LORCAN WAS familiar with the inside of a pleasure house. While travelling these past decades, the need to touch another person often overwhelmed him and the least complicated way of getting what he needed was through coin; it didn't shame him to do so when necessary.

The flash houses of Dublin were unique in the Empire, distinguishing themselves by their brazen existence; they plied their trade openly, in full view of the law. But compared to the houses of sin in the far east, a Dublin flash house was almost tame. The brothels on Mecklenburg were conveniently arranged by street number - the higher the number, the flashier the house - so the number of this house set it above most and would cater to an exclusive clientele of rich businessmen, lords and even, if rumour was to be believed, the occasional royal. The more expensive houses also meant the girls would be free from disease. No guarantee, of course, and the place looked well past its prime.

Upon gaining admittance, Lorcan paused in the hallway, ignoring the glowering brute who'd opened the door. Lorcan was sure that the man hadn't appreciated his tone, but he had calculated it to be arrogant, and it had served its purpose well.

The house bully was huge, with ham-sized fists, but Lorcan swore he'd slice the man's face off if he didn't quit staring. It took conscious effort for Lorcan to remain in control. He closed his eyes to calm himself, focusing first on the rhythmic ticking of the grandfather clock nearby, then moved his attention to other sounds in the house: music and laughter coming from down the hall, a door opening, and closing somewhere above. Finally, the sounds from outside, vendors and prostitutes hawking their wares, the clip-clopping of hooves as a coach rattled by. He then pulled back to the hallway and allowed his senses to take in his immediate surroundings again. The act of grounding cleared his mind. He felt sharp as the kukri blade sitting snug at his back.

"What are you playing at, mister?" said the muscle.

The man's look was full of distrust, so Lorcan smiled. "Just relaxing the nerves before I go in, friend," he said. His smile broadened, as he considered what he'd see in the brute's eyes should he cut slivers from his flesh and feed them to him.

"Well, none of that strangeness when you're with the girls, or I'll crack your skull." The man shook a fist the size and constitution of a small boulder in front of Lorcan's face to illustrate the point.

"There'll be no trouble from me. You have my word."

The brute grunted and nodded dismissively down the hall.

The noise of revelry increased as Lorcan walked towards a door at the end of the hallway. He pushed it open, and the noise washed over him in a burst of warm air, cigar smoke, sweat, and perfume. Two more strides saw Lorcan in the thick of it, somewhat surprised that the room was almost full. *A busy place indeed!*

A pianist played a lively song, possibly something Russian, on the upright Hartley against the wall; he was using the soft pedal. A portly gentleman sang along as he occupied himself with the girl draped languidly around his neck. A barman distributed drinks with practiced ease from the crowded bar on the opposite side of the room: liquor, wine, beer - anything to keep the customers pleased, and malleable for the girls. If there was ever a mean-spirited drunk, a bully would be there to take charge.

Lorcan made for the bar and ordered a whiskey. He downed it in one and lined up another as he scanned the room for his target. Several unoccupied girls circulated, and

Lorcan focused on them, but none looked familiar. He moved to a place against the wall which looked to be out of the way and from which he could study the room.

He had just settled when she entered from a door opposite. Her hair was a tumble of dark curls, deep brown eyes, and a pale complexion, pretty, in a moody sort of way, and strikingly familiar. *Nemhain...* His heart was being wrenched from his chest. Maybe the long years since Nemhain's death had caused her image to fade in his memory and the resemblance wasn't as close, but to him he gazed upon his deceased wife again. He struggled to resist the urge to go to her.

He watched as she avoided all advances. She clearly had no interest in entertaining anyone here and judging by the amount of drink she fed the plants dotted here and there, she had no intention of getting drunk, either. He wondered what her story was, what turns in life led her to this moment.

A drunken oaf approached her when she had her back turned to dispose of the rest of her drink. He slurred something in her ear as he grabbed between her legs. For a moment, she was shocked, but she recovered swiftly, executing a clever move that unbalanced the unsteady drunkard and dumped what remained in her glass over him.

She apologised right away and, with apparent sincerity, assured him she would be back to help clean up the mess. She slipped into the crowd once more and approached Lorcan's location, unaware he had observed the incident.

"Well played, miss," he said.

She looked at him, a glimmer of fear in her eyes, but that wasn't the whole of it. She was wary too, but he mostly saw the will to fight looking back at him.

Lorcan leaned into her before she either attempted to flee or, more likely, struck him. "I saw you on the street," he said.

A look of confusion from her as she asked, "What?"

"I was on the bridge," he said, and to clarify, added, "I was going to jump in."

A moment more of puzzlement before recognition dawned. "I remember you. That would have been a foolish thing to do. The water is freezing this time of year."

"So I've been told."

A commotion from the direction she'd come from. The drunkard, wine-stained and irate, cast his vengeful gaze about the room. It didn't take long for him to spot her, and his finger pointed in their direction. "There she is," he said.

She turned to him with genuine fear in her eyes, so he did what any gentleman would do, seeing a lady in distress. He offered her his arm. "Perhaps we can take this conversation somewhere more private, miss?" he asked.

Unease, as her eyes flitted between the drunkard's commotion and Lorcan. She was wary, and rightly so. "I can help," he said, and she must have heard the commitment in his voice.

She nodded, barely hesitating. "This way." She linked her arm with his and half dragged him to the door leading to the hallway.

CHAPTER 9
THE PLAN

"Why do you want to help me?" Fea asked the stranger.

She sat perched on the luxurious mattress of the grand four-poster bed, watching him as he peered from the third-story window, scoping out an escape route, she assumed. *God! I'm tired,* she thought. She wanted nothing more than to flop back on the fresh bedding and sink into the depths of dreams. But she couldn't, wouldn't dare; not until she was safely away from the brothel. "Well?" she asked.

The man looked around and she stared at the dark intensity of his eyes. "You remind me of somebody I... cared about," he said.

"Lucky girl," she said, making light of it.

"I believe I was the fortunate one," he said, in a flat, matter-of-fact voice. He crossed from the window to the door and bent his ear to listen. Satisfied, he tested the already locked door again - he'd locked it when they had entered moments before - and turned to look at her as he leaned back against the door.

"Is she the reason you were on the bridge?" Fea asked. Something flashed in his eyes that she couldn't put her finger on. A maelstrom of anger, grief, pain, and weariness.

"The river can wait," he said, forcing a lightness his eyes belied. Fea saw the shadow of genuine pain there and appreciated the effort it took to keep it in check.

Pain was something she was fast growing accustomed to. Her attitude towards him softened, the beginnings of trust. She hopped off the bed faster than expected; the bed being much springier than she was used to, and stumbled as she closed the distance between them. She held out her hand as she introduced herself. "Fea Murrigan," she said.

He had the grace to subdue the smile that twitched at the corner of his mouth. "Lorcan Crowley," he said, enclosing her hand in a firm grip. They shook, a bond of sorts between them.

"What's the plan?" she asked.

Lorcan considered the question before shrugging. "We're too high to jump, and climbing down would be risky without a strong rope," he said.

"That's not encouraging."

"However... it's but a short walk along the landing to the stairs, and two flights down will see us to the front hall-way. A few yards more to the front door..."

"Yes?" she prompted him to continue.

"Our best chance is to walk out of here... and if we're spotted, we run for it."

"Run for it?" she fought to keep incredulity from her voice. "That's your plan?"

He nodded.

"And the man-mountain at the door?" she asked. Fea looked him up and down. "I'm sorry, but there's no way you could beat him."

He showed no signs of being offended. "I've got nothing to lose, and neither have you. We also have the element of surprise, and..." Lorcan reached behind his back and produced a wickedly curved, exotic looking blade. "...I can cut the man-mountain down to size."

His smile sent a shiver up Fea's spine. *What manner of man is this?*

FIACHRA'S NOSTRILS flared mere inches from the filthy ground as he inhaled deeply. It was futile; not a hint of the two young-lings remained amidst the multitude of scents assailing him.

He stood and brushed the grime from his clothing as he scanned the crooked street. By the demeanour of the men and women coming and going, this was where the lower end of the prostitute market was located. The women selling themselves were well past their prime and had experienced every tribulation their trade could throw at them.

Midway along the row of closest houses, a doorway opened and a small, raggedly dressed figure exited alone. The house was rundown, unlike its neighbours, that had at least a cursory sign of being maintained. After a few moments, another older child emerged, also garbed in rags. Neither child had the exact scent he was after, but they were both similar enough for it to warrant further investigation. He pulled up the lapels of his jacket and strode along the cobbled street to the rundown house.

The iron gate hung off its hinges and remained permanently open. Taking the short path past the overgrown patches of garden, he saw nothing of the interior through the windows on either side of the door. The door itself was closed, but unlocked, so he slipped inside.

Within the house, the narrow hallway was mildewy, but he smelled a gathering of young-lings close by. He padded to the door in front of him and listened. His ears and snout elongated to the beginnings of their wolf form. With nourishment came strength, which gave him more control over his form, despite the silver shackle.

From behind the door, he picked up whispers without making out the words. A handful of distinct scents came from the room. One was that of one of the young-lings he sought.

Without announcement, he crashed through the door-way, taking it off its hinges. He roared in the entrance as the door slammed to the floor. He filled the room with a growl that elicited comical jumps from those within. "Ahhhh," screamed the majority, but a taller, braver one came forward. "What the hell, mister?"

Most of them were to his right, the screamers, and the brave boy. To the left lay a crumpled heap as far away from the others as possible. That was the one he sought.

Just as he was about to go to her, someone interrupted him. "This is our place, mister," said the brave one as he approached Fiachra.

Fiachra turned, bemused, anticipating the fear his half-transformed face would bring. But the boy didn't register fear, nor anything like it. *What a face!* thought Fiachra as the boy closed on him. *He could be kindred, only with rodents instead of wolf.*

"Get out, before we make you," said the rat-boy.

"Yeah, get out," echoed a younger boy who came to stand by rat-boy's left side. A larger boy moved to the right and puffed his chest out as he folded his arms.

Fiachra welcomed them, like the wolf welcomed the lamb, but he gave them a chance. "Stand back, lads," he said in a low growl. He flicked his eyes to the girl lying on the floor by the opposite wall. "It's the wee girl I want."

"She's not yours to take, dog-breath," said the rat-boy.

His accomplices snickered. Their reaction confused Fiachra. By rights, they should run for their lives from him. *Too stupid to have the sense to run, but I'll show them fear.*

He removed his jacket and threw it to one side, then removed his shirt too, revealing his naked torso caked in dried blood. Before the shirt hit the refuse strewn floor, his transformation to wolf form was underway. The sight rooted the gathered boys in place, eyes bulging from sockets and mouths agape as his skin stretched and tore as the muscles beneath transmogrified. He pushed further than he had yet done, testing his limits.

Once his teeth were out, Fiachra wasted no time. He lunged at the rat-boy and bit down on his face. At the last moment, the boy stepped back, but not soon enough. Fiachra's savage teeth caught the skin of the rat-boy's face and ripped it away, leaving surprised eyes set in a glistening, muscled skull. Fiachra was convinced it was an improvement.

The former rat-faced boy screamed and turned to his companions. The sight of his destroyed face galvanised them into movement, each falling backwards in a different direction. Their eyes didn't leave their friends'.

The screaming was causing pain to build in Fiachra's temple. He stepped in and pulled the boy to him, biting his neck. The scream cut off as Fiachra consumed his vocal chords. *Blessed relief!*

Fiachra cast aside the still twitching body and lunged at the larger of the two accomplices. Straddling the lad, he went straight for the heart, first slicing away the rags that covered the chest, then ripping aside the flesh that covered the ribcage. The lad's bones cracked as Fiachra opened him barehanded to reveal his beating heart. He consumed it and luxuriated in the feeling of it beating as he swallowed it whole.

The last assailant had gained enough senses to break for the door, but Fiachra bounded after him and snapped his ankle off in one bite. The lad tumbled to the ground with an agonised cry, but he continued to crawl for the door. Fiachra severed his spine at the base of his skull with a snap of his jaws, and the lad went limp.

Fiachra dragged the lad to the wall and propped him there, where he could watch as Fiachra finished his meal. It would keep his heart fresh, the best possible way to eat one, in Fiachra's opinion.

The girl! With all the commotion, Fiachra forgot about his purpose for being there. Looking for her now, he saw that the bundle which lay against the opposite wall was gone. "Where are you, little one?" asked Fiachra in a pleasant voice. The silence hung heavy in the air.

Fiachra didn't care about the girl at all, if he was being honest with himself. He would pick up her scent again or he wouldn't. But only after he'd finished his meal. He bent to the open torso, which lay in the middle of the floor, and feasted on the remaining organs as the wide, teary eyes of his dessert watched on.

~

TOMMY WAS EXHAUSTED as he sat in the crawlspace between the brothel walls. The horror of the previous night haunted him and had caused a fitful night's sleep in the orphan house. Worry about Margaret played its part too and he willed time to move faster so that he could be with her again. He believed the house was a safe-haven, and he thought she would be okay as long as she kept their takings out of sight of the other children. However, he knew that other darkness stalked the city streets.

Tommy was a wall-rat at the flash house, employed by Madam Arnott herself. It was his job to listen to conversations that went on during the night between important men and the women they tumbled. At the end of his shift, he reported what he'd heard to the madam herself and nobody else.

On a normal day, Tommy was one of the best, but on this occasion, he spent more time fighting his lowering eyelids than listening like he was supposed to. He prayed he wouldn't fall asleep and snore, as was his habit. That would be an end to the brothel's reputation as a discreet house to visit and inevitably be an end to Tommy, too. The madam was known for being unforgiving and brutal when she needed to set an example. So, he fought sleep like his life depended on it, moving carefully through the spaces under the floorboards and between the walls when the risk of staying still was too great.

He had just changed position for the tenth time in as many minutes when he heard the door to the room he listened at open and close, and a moment later the lock clicked. He drifted off again, then focused when he heard the word 'plan'. Certain words and phrases stood out in this line of work, piqued the attention, grabbed you. There could be something important here.

Tommy shifted again to bring his ear closer to the sounds of the room. He closed his eyes to focus, slowed his breathing so it would not interfere with what was being said. As an extra precaution against unwanted sleep, he felt for a sharp piece of wood along the wall, picked it off and jammed in into his leg. The pain brought tears to his eyes, but it was worth it; Madam Arnott would have his head if he missed anything important.

The talk in the room was unusual. There was no hint of the pillow talk Tommy was used to hearing. Instead, the talk was of escape. The fool was suggesting he and the girl walk out of the front door and take on Seamus if necessary. Tommy shook his head, amazed at the foolish play. *Seamus will take his head off.* Madam Arnott said to report anything out of the ordinary and this certainly qualified.

Tommy moved from his listening spot, careful not to make any noise that would give away his presence, but quick enough that he'd get his report to the madam's ear in time. There was something familiar in the man's voice, but Tommy couldn't place it. It was highly likely that one of the regulars had become completely infatuated with one of the girls. *Strange that she doesn't sound familiar.* Tommy thought he knew all the women who worked in the brothel's rooms. Regardless, Madam Arnott would be pleased with his information, and he might even receive a fine bonus. *One step closer to getting out of this shithole,* he thought. *And one step closer to seeing Margaret safe.*

~

LORCAN OPENED the door and poked his head out to check the second-floor landing. All was clear. He opened the door and stepped out, with Fea close beside him. He could tell by the tight grip on his arm that she was nervous, but a quick look showed she hid it well.

Every instinct within him cried out to run, but he kept

his pace even and made sure his air was casual. A leisurely walk to the top of the stairs and they made their way down.

On the next landing, on the first floor, they encountered another prostitute, so Lorcan tipped his hat and smiled at her. She paid them no heed, and they walked the short distance to the top of the last stairs. From their position, they had a complete view of the bottom of the stairs, where it met the hallway close to the front door. They were in luck; the man-mountain wasn't there.

"Quickly," said Lorcan, and picked up the pace. Fea matched it without hesitation. When they reached the bottom, the way was still clear. Lorcan thought this peculiar, but they were too far along the path to change it now. Their feet pattered on the tiles as they ran, skidding the last inches. Lorcan found the catch and attempted to disengage it, but it wouldn't budge.

A gasp beside him. Fea raised her hand to cover her mouth as she watched behind them.

Lorcan turned, but a gigantic figure barrelled into him and knocked his breath out. The force was immense as he hit the ground. Trapped under a suffocating weight, he struggled to rise. He could only move an inch, but after a moment, the weight lifted.

Lorcan spun and saw Fea clinging to the enormous man's back, clawing at his neck. The man reached back with one hand and pulled her off him like she was a child. He threw her into the wall and Fea dropped to the floor, unmoving.

The man-mountain turned back to Lorcan; his face made more menacing by the red scratch marks. "Thought you'd get away with another one of me girls, did ye?"

"I-," started Lorcan, but the man-mountain raised a hand with a leather wrapped stick, then swiped down onto

Lorcan's head. The floor dropped away and Lorcan fell into darkness.

~

MADAM ARNOTT ENTERED the hallway through the door to the back of the house. Seamus towered above the thief, who lay on the floor next to the front door. The man was unconscious and bleeding from a head wound, but Seamus raised the cudgel for another strike.

"That's enough!" she said, causing the large man to start. "We don't want him dead... not yet."

"Yes, ma'am," said Seamus, immediately subservient.

Madam Arnott moved closer to them and saw the girl lying on the floor next to the stairs. *I should have known it would be the new girl,* she thought. This was not the first trouble the girl had caused in a handful of hours. "Is she dead?" she asked.

Seamus stooped to listen at her mouth. After a minute, he got up, head shaking. "Still breathing, ma'am," he said.

"Good. I would like her to suffer for the trouble she's caused."

A rhythmic pounding on the front door interrupted their conversation. It was quite unlike the usual furtive rapping to gain admittance.

Seamus looked at her questioningly and she *tsked.* "Don't stand there. Open it."

He sprang into action and dragged the thief to one side. Opening the door a crack, he opened his mouth with a quick response formed, but smacked his mouth closed and slammed the door shut again. A look of fear spread upon his face, which the madam found intriguing. She didn't know of a lot that would phase the man; he hadn't the imagination for it. "The Sisters," he said, all colour gone from his face.

That would explain it, thought Madam Arnott. The Sisters were unnerving at the best of times. She could only imagine the fear they instilled in those more... impressionable. "Take him to the cellar," she said. When Seamus didn't move, she added an impatient note to her voice. "Quickly now. I'll deal with the Sisters."

Seamus took the thief beneath the arms and hoisted him over his shoulder, giving no obvious sign of strain. He hurried through the door she'd entered by moments before. That left her and the unconscious new girl in the hallway.

Before opening the door, the madam hid her emotions. As Seamus had said, the two Sisters stood motionless on the top step, their faces obscured by porcelain and unnerving eyes peering out. "Afternoon, Sister. To what do I owe this pleasure?"

"Pleasure," said the one on the right, savouring the word.

"You have something that belongs to us," said the other.

Both Sisters were identical. Height, build, clothing, and porcelain mask had no variance between the two, to denote seniority or rank, if those concepts existed in their order. Madam Arnott chose the more vociferous Sister to direct her response. "I assure you, if there is anything belonging to the Sisters within my house, it is unintended," she said. "What is the nature of this thing?"

The Sister on the right cocked her head to one side as though listening. Madam Arnott strained to listen too but could hear nothing above the sounds from the street.

"She is close," the right-hand Sister whispered.

"You have a girl within these walls who belongs to us," said the left-hand Sister.

"Old blood," added the one on the right.

Madam Arnott had a distinct impression that the right one's words irritated the left one. *Interesting,* she thought. "Can you describe this girl of the old blood?" said the madam. She deliberately added the right-hand Sister's phrase to see if it elicited a response.

The left-hand Sister remained statue-still for a few breaths' length before gliding the short distance that separated her from the madam.

Unconsciously, Madam Arnott moved backwards, allowing the Sister to cross the threshold and enter the hallway.

The Sister looked to the right and zoned in on the crumpled form of the new girl. "Take her," said the left-hand Sister and the other Sister entered and lifted the girl in her arms with little more effort than Seamus showed when he threw her there. She carried the girl from the hallway into the street, leaving Madam Arnott with the Sister who was clearly in charge.

"You will get but one warning. If the Sisters ask, you will give. Do not test us again," said the Sister. She turned and glided out of the front door without looking back.

Madam Arnott waited until the two had moved away before shutting and locking the door. She leaned back against the door, somewhat relieved. Sounds of revelry came from within the house again, as though the Sisters had muted them. She gave herself a few minutes to recover, then marched confidently down the hallway in the direction Seamus had taken the thief. She had questions for the man and, one way or another, he would answer.

Fiachra bounded through the labyrinthine maze of alleys on his way back to the ash-pit dump, still half-transformed. He was full of the flesh of his recent feast, and he rejoiced. He'd forgotten the difference between a youthful meal, albeit malnourished, and that of diseased flesh.

The last boy, the one he'd paralyzed and made to watch him devour his companions, had been a fine meal indeed, with flesh transformed into a delicacy by the buildup of dread. He had devoured half the boy's organs before the youngster knew he was dead. Fiachra's strength was back, and as close to its peak as the silver band would allow.

With a burst of motion, he kicked from ground to wall and leaped from one side of the alley to the other almost too fast for the men and women who walked its crooked ways. In no time at all, he was back at the dump.

Launching himself from the wall opposite, he smoothly landed amid the foul debris and got to work locating the trail of the man who had also been present at the recent killings. It didn't take long before he found it, leading off in the opposite direction to the two children. With the enhanced sense of smell that resulted from his quality meal, he caught another scent. It was ancient and raised the hackles on the back of his neck. *What are you bitches getting me into now?* No wonder they had him to do their dirty work.

No matter, he thought. *Dirty work was work, nonetheless.* He wasted no more time in thinking about it. He had succumbed to his baser instincts over the past hours, and now he focused. He had to provide something for the Sisters, if for no other reason but to give himself more time to plan his escape from them.

Nose close to the ground, he loped away, following the man's trail.

CHAPTER 10
ESCAPE

Lorcan rose in the early morning to find Nemhain's side of the bed empty. A quick check on Cormac's room and the boy was missing, too. "Where have you two gone?" he muttered as he descended the stairs and made for the kitchen. He'd murder for some food.

Catherine had her back to him as he entered, preparing something on the stove.

"Morning, Catherine," he said.

"Morning, Master Crowley. I hope you slept well," she said. A familiar greeting.

"Too well, in truth. Have you seen Nemhain and Cormac?"

"Aye, they recently departed." She turned, brandishing a pan on which freshly cooked eggs were ready. "The mistress said they were off for a walk. She left you a note."

Lorcan hardly heard her, so surprised was he by her state. The woman's neck was open in a gaping gash which oozed blackened blood. Globs of it dropped into the pan and sizzled amongst the eggs.

"The note," Catherine said again, seeing his open-mouthed stare.

He looked down at the table to where she indicated and saw a folded parchment. He picked it up and opened it, seeing his wife's familiar handwriting:

My Dearest Lorcan.
Forgive me for not being able to suffer this world any longer,
Forgive me for not being able to take my next path alone.
We must keep our blood from them.
Love,
Nemhain

He had to read it a second time before the meaning sank in. Thoughts of Catherine's wound forgotten, he grabbed her shoulders. "Which way did they go, Catherine!?" he shouted at her.

She backed away from him, terrified by his intensity, the flow of thick blood increasing from her gaping neck wound. "I don't know, master. She spoke of the river."

At the mention of water, he turned and ran full tilt for the front door, stopping just long enough to don his boots and grab a coat.

On the street, he pulled on his coat as he jogged north, past Trinity College, towards the Liffey. As he came in sight of the Sackville Street bridge, he saw them. "Nemhain!" he called, but he was too far away to be heard. The street was too busy, and the noise of the trams and carriages didn't help.

He stepped out on the street proper, heedless of the oncoming traffic, and sprinted to his wife and child, calling, "Nemhain! Cormac!"

His son looked back, but his wife pushed his face away from

Lorcan and towards the river. She lifted the boy to sit on the stone wall, then climbed up to sit next to him.

Lorcan increased his pace and shouted again, despite being out of breath. "Cormac! Nemhain!"

Nemhain glanced his way then, and he was close enough to see her gentle smile. She raised a hand and waved to him as though she was out on an excursion and would be back to see him soon. She held Cormac close to her in a mother's hug. Then she leaned over and pulled the two of them off the bridge.

As they fell, Cormac turned to look at Lorcan, fear written on his face. "Dada!" he cried before they both disappeared from sight.

Lorcan ran like he had never run in his life. He got to the stone wall that lined the bridge and, without hesitation, he dived over it, following them. Seconds later he hit the freezing water and went under, the shock of it almost driving the breath from him. He held onto it because letting it go was death for him and his family.

Casting around in the murky river water, he could see but a few feet in front. He thought he saw a pale shape beneath him, Nemhain's dress perhaps, and swam after it. It remained just out of his reach, but he wouldn't, couldn't, give up. He swam deeper.

His fingers told him when he reached the riverbed. He cast about in the filth, but there was nothing. He swam to left and right, running out of air, but he was desperate to glimpse them. Where are you? His mind raged. The freezing water sapped the warmth from him as his deprived lungs protested and pushed him to instinctively take a breath. Then it occurred to him not to bother. What reason was there for him to go back to the surface without his wife and child? There was no reason. He relaxed his body and allowed the water to embrace him as he breathed it deep into his lungs.

LORCAN AWOKE SPLUTTERING from the freezing water which had been thrown over him. His mind was still in his drowning dream, his lungs still taking a last watery breath as the river welcomed him with its icy embrace. He felt disoriented, and it took him long moments to realise that he was somewhere dark and damp, and that he was freshly soaked, but no longer about to meet his maker. Not that he believed much in that sort of thing.

"Wakey, wakey," said a gruff voice from beyond the fitful flame of an oil lamp that sat on a crate directly before him.

Looking straight at the light caused Lorcan to squint as pain lanced through his head. He remembered the brief altercation after the botched escape attempt and tried to move from his seat. He discovered that he was bound in place. *By rough ropes, if I'm not mistaken.* It wasn't the first time he'd been bound in such a fashion. He sensed that he was tied up alone, so it begged a question. "Where's the girl?" He wished his voice sounded stronger.

"Far from where you'll get her," said the voice. "Far from where anyone can help her now." This elicited an unpleasant laugh that Lorcan didn't like one bit.

"What do you want with me?" he asked.

"The madam has questions," said the voice. "So 'ave I."

From out of the blackness came a hand, the slap taking Lorcan by surprise. It was a leisurely blow, but it rocked him. Lorcan figured it was the man-mountain for surely nobody else could deliver such a strike with so little effort.

"What did you do with the other girl?" asked the man-mountain.

Lorcan hadn't a notion what the man was talking

about. "I know of no other girl," said Lorcan. Another blow, but Lorcan was prepared for it and turned his head as it landed. It still rattled him, causing specks of light to dot his vision.

"Try again," said the man-mountain.

Lorcan cast his mind about to figure out what the man referred to. As far as he could recall, the only person he spoke to in the brothel had been this monster and Fea Murrigan. Since he'd set foot in the city, he'd had little meaningful contact with anybody since taking the coat from the man at the docks. Even in the síbín he'd kept to himself. There'd been the two children who led him to the daemon in the alleyway who'd been doing that to... surely not. "Can you describe the woman you speak of?" he asked.

The man-mountain spoke in a voice that was almost gentle. "Kate O'Connor is a grand lass; one you'd be proud to settle down with. She has brown hair and green eyes and was wearing respectable clothes last night when she left here." A deep sigh and in almost a whisper, "I should have followed her like I do sometimes." The man coughed as though clearing a lump from his throat before continuing. "She didn't show for her shift tonight, and there's no sign of her at her digs." The voice turned hard. "But then you show up and try to take another. Right from under me nose."

A hard blow shot out and struck Lorcan, once again catching him off guard. His world went black for an indeterminate length of time. His left ear buzzed when he surfaced. As his vision cleared, a rectangle of light appeared in the ceiling as a trapdoor opened. *I'm in a cellar,* he thought, as a woman of distinction descended the wooden steps. Halfway down, she stopped and took in the scene. "That's enough, Seamus," she said, in English leaning heavily into a French accent.

"Yes, ma'am," said Seamus.

She descended the remaining steps and stood behind the lantern light alongside her lackey. A moment of quiet observation, perhaps waiting for him to break the silence. Lorcan knew better than that.

After a full minute, the madam broke the silence. "So. Who are you and why do you steal my girls?" she asked.

Lorcan decided to be straight with her. Perhaps she would appreciate his honesty and he could still save Fea. She might even allow him to pay for her freedom. "In truth, I saw her pass by this morning and followed her here. She reminded me of my late wife," he said.

"You expect me to believe that?" asked the madam in a flat tone.

"It's the truth," he said.

"Don't believe him," said Seamus.

"Silence," she said, cutting him off, before adding, "Leave us."

"But it's not safe, Ma'am."

"I am more than capable of looking after myself in the company of one beaten and bound romantic," she said.

Seamus huffed and stomped up the wooden steps like a chastened child. The steps creaked and groaned in protest, but they held.

When Seamus was gone, the madam stepped from beyond the lantern and took a seat on the box on which it stood. Lorcan took her in for the first time and saw that she was beautiful in a timeless way and possessed that confident air of women who had broken free of the chains society had placed around them, usually as a betrothal. "What is your name?"

"Lorcan. Lorcan Crowley. And you?"

"They call me Madam Arnott here. That will do for now," she said.

"Pleased to meet you, Madam Arnott," he said. "I'd gladly shake your hand should you free mine."

She laughed at that, in genuine humour. "I'm sure you would," she said. She leaned down and took something from the floor. "I'm sure you would also like this?" It was his kukri knife. Madam Arnott took it from its sheathe and looked at the blade with great admiration. "Well looked after," she said.

He didn't respond, just watched her handling the blade.

"Now, Mr Crowley, I will ask you again," she said as she tested the blade on her finger. It sliced into her flesh and drew a bead of blood. Madam Arnott smiled and licked the blood from her hand. She turned to Lorcan, and for the first time he noticed something unhinged beyond the light in her eyes. "Why do you steal my girls?"

Before he could answer, she swiped out with his kukri in a slashing motion. He violently kicked backwards and felt the chair topple. Without his hands to catch himself, he was at the mercy of gravity, but he kept his head forward so as not to sustain another blow; there'd been far too much of that already.

She cackled; a sound incongruous to the beautiful lady but right in line with the madness he'd glimpsed a moment before. From above, he heard a cacophonous uproar. Shouting and the noise of fighting.

"What now?" asked the madam, more to herself than to him, Lorcan thought. He kept quiet, thinking she'd believe him unconscious. "Rest there, Mr Crowley. I will be back once I've dealt with this."

He heard steel on wood. His kukri being placed down? He could only hope. Then she ascended the stairs and left him alone in the basement. He trashed about on the floor, straining at his bonds and the rough chair they tied him to. Either they would give, or his limbs would, he thought grimly.

MADAM ARNOTT HAD GREETED with delight Tommy's news of the escape plan, and, as he'd hoped, she'd given him a fat purse of coin. So delighted was she that she insisted on him watching the fruition of his good work. "It will be a valuable part of your education to see the consequences of going against me," she said. He was unsure if this was a warning to him; knowing the madam, it probably was.

He had to admit; he was curious to get a look at the man who would go against Madam Arnott, but when he recognised the man, the blood drained from his face. *The man who helped us last night!* He tried to open the door through which he had peeked, but someone yanked him back.

"What do you think you're doing?" asked a threatening voice from right by his ear. He'd forgotten all about the man who stood guard at the door - there on the off-chance the gentleman got past Seamus and tried to escape through the back of the house. Each door off the hallway had a guard stationed correspondingly.

"But he's not the one who took Kate," said Tommy in a whisper.

The guard shrugged. "Doesn't matter. He's trying to make off with the madam's property. He'd be dead no matter what you say."

The injustice almost overwhelmed Tommy. He knew that the man was innocent, having seen him attempt to rescue Kate the previous night, and when he failed, he made sure the daemon couldn't do the same to anyone else. *What can I do?* Tommy was no fool and realised he could do nothing at that moment, so he'd bid his time. He'd watched the trap being sprung and the man getting caught. He watched in silence as the madam arrived and saved the man's life from a fatal blow from Seamus, and watched nervously as Seamus carried him away to the cellar. Finally, he saw the two awful Sisters arrive and carry away the girl, for God knew what evil purpose.

The madam then returned. "You've earned yourself a favour from me, Tommy," she'd said, all smiles. "What would you ask of me?"

He wasn't falling for it. "Nothing, Madam Arnott, miss," he'd said. "I was jus' doin' me job."

"That's a good lad," she'd said, smile fading as she rose. "Well, back to work then."

"Yes, ma'am," he said and climbed back into the gap between the walls to listen to more conversations between the women of the house and the men who paid for them. It took him an hour or two of deep thought before he came up with his own plan. He mapped out the narrow walkways between the walls in his mind and chose a route that would bring him past as many rooms as possible before reaching the kitchen. Then he waited until the busy hour just after dinnertime.

At the appointed hour, he moved as quickly as possible through the spaces, making an awful racket by banging on the walls and shouting, "The madam is listening! The madam hears it all!" He left in his wake a cacophonous outcry of irate voices. "What's that?" and "What is the meaning of this?!" and "Who spoke?" followed by variations on "This will be the end of this establishment, mark my words!"

Tommy knew this was the end of his employment there and the small part of him that wasn't in fear of his life from the madam's retribution was joyous at finally being free of the place. He had enough money saved to take himself and Margaret away from the city. They could make a fresh start in Cork. He'd heard it was wonderful down there.

He slipped out of the walls by a hidden door in the madam's office at the back of the house. The kitchen was just outside the door, so he opened it a crack and surveyed the trapdoor into the cellar.

The front part of the house echoed with the growing noises of outraged men, accompanied by sounds of physical violence to match their harsh words. A moment later, the madam ascended from the cellar, looking furious. She ran past the office door and slammed the door into the hallway behind her. Her raised voice joined the many arguments.

Tommy seized the opportunity to slip out of the office and dart across the kitchen to the trapdoor. He entered the cellar and paused until his eyes adjusted. He spotted the shape struggling on the floor, and bounding down the steps, he raced over. With his hands under the back of the chair, he strained to lift the man upright.

"The knife," said the man.

Tommy followed the man's eyes to the box with the lantern. A curved blade lay beside the dim light source. Giving up his struggle with the chair, Tommy retrieved the knife, careful not to cut himself on the blade. The knife was razor sharp and cut through the rough rope that held the man with ease.

Once Lorcan's arms were free, Tommy handed the knife over to him to take care of his feet. Tommy ran back up the steps and peered into the kitchen. The way was clear, and he could hear the raised voices still fighting in the hallway.

He didn't think the madam's bullies would let that go on for much longer. "Come on!" he hissed.

"I'm coming," said Lorcan, and hobbled into view. "My legs have needles and pins from the rope."

Tommy beckoned him forward, and Lorcan climbed the steps to join him at the edge of the opening.

"Is there a back way out?" asked Lorcan.

"This way," said Tommy.

He crossed the large kitchen and passed the door to the larder, then down three steps and around a corner to a dark corridor which led to a closed door. A bully boy sat on a stool just inside it. Tommy put his hand on Lorcan's chest to stop him. "Wait here," he said and turned the corner alone.

The bully boy sat up straighter when he first saw Tommy, but relaxed when it wasn't anyone important. "What do you want?" asked the bully boy.

"There's trouble in the house. They've all gone mad! Madam wants everyone to help. Said I could watch the door."

The bully boy looked doubtful, but Tommy added, "She said to hurry. I won't let anyone in."

The bully boy nodded and rushed past where Lorcan crouched in the larder. Lorcan stepped out when it was clear and joined the boy. "Quick thinking," he said.

Tommy almost didn't hear him as he busied himself with opening the back door. After a bit of fiddling with the lock mechanism, he got it open. The frigid evening air was a welcome blast for Tommy, and he heard Lorcan sigh in appreciation. Neither of them needed prompting but stepped out into the darkness of the backyard. Thirty feet away was a stone wall at head height on Lorcan. They ran to it, and Lorcan lifted the boy onto it without prompting.

Then he took a few steps back and ran at the wall, hoisting himself up beside Tommy.

At the back door, angry voices erupted. "There he is!"

Tommy was wide eyed and bore a worried expression, but when he looked at Lorcan, all he saw was a toothy grin. "Nice night for a chase, eh, lad?" Then the man jumped into the yard that backed onto the houses on Mecklenburg street. He raised his arms for Tommy. "Down you come."

Tommy jumped, allowing the big man to catch him and guide him to the street.

"Lead the way," said the man.

Tommy headed off in search of Margaret with Lorcan in tow.

MARGARET HID in the narrow lane mere yards from the house where the monster ate the mean boys. She'd snuck out the back door after escaping the room while he ate Ratso and his two stupid friends. Tommy said she shouldn't call them names, but she didn't care, and anyway, there wasn't anything they could do to her now.

Pain lanced into her side, and she winced but fought back the tears. She didn't want to make noise, even though she'd been hiding in the alley for what seemed like a long time. She thought the monster would have found her by now if it was going to.

She was hungry, and so thirsty that the disgusting puddles of muddy rainwater and refuse looked appealing. Her stomach growled, and she tensed her muscles to muffle the sound, but the action only served in causing more pain. She couldn't hold back the tears that time. *I need to find Tommy,* she thought. Her anxiety grew as she remained uncertain about the pain's origin. *Tommy will know what to do.*

She threw off the pile of rubbish she'd burrowed under, trying not to think of the awful smells and what the cold squishy sensation on her hands was.

Beaver Street, outside the alley, was getting busier as the afternoon wore on, and all sorts scurried here and there. Margaret paused at the mouth of the alley and watched the comings and goings for a few minutes before stepping into the flow. She kept close to the buildings and away from the road as she walked towards Mecklenburg Street and the place Tommy worked. It had to be close to his finishing time, so she would wait outside the front door for him.

Keeping her head down, she navigated the street full of busy adults, invisible to them because of her size and her low stature. Orphan children went unseen unless they'd brought attention to themselves. The only one she had to worry about was the monster.

She slowed when she reached the intersection of Mecklenburg and Beaver streets and surveyed left and right. She was about to turn left towards her objective when a cry came from the right. "Margaret?!"

"Tommy?" she said, confused why he approached from the wrong direction. She spotted him ducking and weaving to avoid traffic as he crossed the road. Behind him came the man from the previous night who'd killed the evil man. A carriage thundered towards them, and she thought it might run them into the ground, but the man turned towards it and barked a command that caused the horses to rear away from him.

Tommy ran to her and picked her up, hugging her close, but he let her down when she cried out in pain. "What's wrong?" he said.

"Hello again, little lady," said the man as he arrived beside Tommy.

"She's hurt," said Tommy.

"Let me see?" The man guided them to the relative peace of a nearby doorway and kneeled beside her. "Where does it hurt?" he asked, as gentle as you like.

Margaret pointed to her side, where the last dart of pain still echoed.

The man raised his hands to her, but stopped before touching her. "May I, miss?" he asked.

Margaret gave a small nod as she bit her lip in anticipation. His hands pressed where she'd shown and she winced, but tried to be strong now that both Tommy's and the man's eyes were upon her.

He pushed all around her side before taking his hands away. "You're very brave," said the man, not an ounce of jest in his voice.

Margaret nervously smiled at him.

"I think nothing is broken, but you might have bruised a bone," he said. "We'll take it easy as we get out of here."

Tommy looked at her, all serious then, and asked in a soft voice, "What happened, Margaret? Who did it?"

Margaret looked down at her feet, then up at his clear blue eyes. "It was Ratso and his pals," she said and saw the anger rise in her brother.

"I'll kill them," said Tommy. He turned back towards Beaver Street.

"No!" shouted Margaret, loud enough to make a couple passing close by jump in fright, then curse at her. Lorcan growled at them, and they moved along.

"Why not?" asked Tommy.

"They're dead," she said, simply.

"What?"

"A monster came looking for us, Tommy, or what we took from Katie..." she looked to Lorcan, "... and the evil man. Ratso robbed me and they kicked me a few times, then left me alone. Then the monster came and ate off Ratso's face and all their insides."

She paled as she recalled the monster eating the boys, but continued. "When he was busy opening up the last one, I snuck out and hid under the rubbish in the alley. I only just came out when you saw me."

The man and Tommy looked at her as though not believing her.

"I swear, Tommy. He kilt them and 'et them."

"You said he was looking for you and Tommy?" asked the man.

"He said he only wanted me when Ratso and his friends started on him."

The man was deep in thought. Then he looked at the two of them before addressing Tommy. "Thank you for helping me, Tommy. I fear that would have been the end of me. But now we must part ways."

"I couldn't leave you there," Tommy said. "Not after you tried to help Kate."

"Aye. A pity I didn't get to her sooner," he said. His face hardened as he thought of something. "There's another woman who needs my help, but I don't know where to start."

"The Sisters took her," said Tommy.

Margaret gasped. She had witnessed the Sisters taking women and children from the streets to the laundry. It terrified her that they never saw them again. "Not the Sisters, Tommy," she said from behind the small hand covering her mouth.

"The Sisters?" asked the man.

"They're the nuns in the laundry, mister," said Margaret. "Nobody comes back from there, not ever."

"Surely you've seen them," said Tommy.

Margaret thought Tommy was thinking about what she was. Either the man was telling lies, or he lived in a hole in the ground for as long as she was alive.

"I've been away from Dublin and Ireland for decades," he said, perhaps reading the doubt on their faces. "I've not heard of these Sisters or the laundry. Where is it?"

"Close to here," said Margaret. "I can show you." She reached up and took his hand, guiding him down the street towards the flash house he'd just escaped from.

He stopped her gently. "Is there another way? One that doesn't pass by Mecklenburg Street."

"It's longer," she said and shrugged. Turning back the way they'd come from, she led them through the busy street.

"Why do they wear those masks?" asked Lorcan. They were positioned across the street from the laundry and watched as two more of the Sisters glided through the main door.

"Because they're monsters," said Margaret.

Not more monsters, thought Lorcan. He still didn't know what to make of the girl's story of a monster eating children. It sounded like a children's nursery story. "If their faces look anything like their hands, then they'd be fierce-ugly cunts," said Tommy.

"Tommy!" said Margaret.

"Well, it's the truth! James Dunne said one of them grabbed him when he stole a loaf of bread last year and the hand was dark and shrivelled up like a bog man. She had sharp black talons, and the grip was so strong it almost ripped his arm off. He said he still has marks from where she grabbed him."

"That James Dunne is the biggest liar," said Margaret. "I wouldn't believe a word of it."

"He showed us the mark," said Tommy. "It looked like a hand mark."

"And these Sisters, these nuns, take women and children off the streets to work in there?" asked Lorcan.

"Yeah," said both children in unison.

"What about the authorities?" asked Lorcan.

The children looked at him as though he were simple. He supposed it was a stupid question. He had seen no signs of the Constabulary on the streets of Monto. Not since he'd been here. While there were many soldiers, they functioned more as customers than a united force. "Point taken," he said. *What will I do?* He had to get into that laundry and free Fea. That was a given. He'd already committed to it. But he felt a certain amount of responsibility to the two orphans, and the tale of a monster bothered him greatly. Maybe he was being stalked too, most likely by a savage man rather that something monstrous. Men were capable of just about anything. He knew that from experience.

Something whispered in his mind, a reminder he was sure, rather than an actual entity. *Feed me...* Between these nuns and whatever stalked them, he would need all the help he could get. *The staff.* He'd left it in his old home on Dawson Street that morning, disgusted at the carnage it had caused. He knew he was no angel, but the slaughter he'd committed in the house had been beyond anything he'd ever done. *They deserved it,* he thought. He wouldn't argue that point. "I need to fetch something from my home," he said to the children, shying away from naming the staff specifically. He didn't want to scare them.

"Can we come?" asked the girl.

She gave him a doe-eyed look that he tried to resist for a second, but he gave up with a sigh. "If you do as I say," he said. *Children!*

The girl hugged him at the waist, gently, he assumed because of her sore ribs. "Thank you!" she said.

"Yeah. Thanks," said Tommy.

Lorcan nodded as he disentangled himself from the girl's arms. "If I tell either of you to do something, then do it. Don't think about it, just do it. Right?"

"Right!" they said. The girl, Margaret, even gave him a small salute.

"Come on." He led them away from the laundry towards the south side of the city.

CHAPTER II

THE LAUNDRY

Fea stood in the unfamiliar hallway, a silent Sister to either side. She knew from experience that there was no point in speaking to them. They didn't respond to idle chitchat, or gossip, or anything that wasn't functional language.

She had regained consciousness in the arms of one of the Sisters, being carried through the streets of Monto. At first, not knowing what was happening, she struggled. After receiving a hard slap, she relaxed into the ride. She had thought the sight of her in a Sister's arms would be a humorous one for the street's denizens, but all she got were looks of pity, when the looks weren't full of fear. She guessed many had suffered at the Sister's hands before.

At one point in their journey, a crow swooped close and screeched furiously at the Sister carrying her. The other Sister swatted at it, the sound of her hand cutting through the air just missing the target.

"Stay away, little brother," she had said, for which she received another hard skelp. She didn't regret it. The crows and ravens were always good to her; she'd not pay them back by causing them any harm.

Once they'd entered the laundry, they placed her on the ground and directed her up the stairs, then down the corridor, to the doorway she stood before. She'd been there for hours and if she had to stand for an hour more, she was positive she'd collapse and be damned what they'd do to her.

As though sensing how close she was to the end of her endurance, a gravelly voice came from behind the closed door. "Enter."

The Sisters moved to each side of her and took her by the arms, half dragging her through the door she'd stared at for half the evening. The room had sparse furnishings, but the items that were present gave an impression of wealth. This didn't surprise Fea, having spent most of her late childhood in a nunnery run by the same order. The prominent feature of the room was the large desk adjacent to the densely curtained windows. The desk boasted a rich, dark wood that almost appeared black, contrasting beautifully with the inlaid wine leather top.

From behind the desk, The Mother watched. Unmoving, eyes glimmering from behind her onyx mask, the opposite of those worn by the Sisters. They led her to the desk, the sound of her footsteps echoing in the empty room. "You found her," said the Mother in a flat tone.

"Yes," said one of the Sisters, and left it at that.

"We tracked her to a brothel," said the other Sister, expanding on it.

The Mother was silent, and it surprised Fea when she noticed a nervous shift from the second Sister. *She's more nervous than I am,* she thought. *That would be impossible.* Fea had never met The Mother before, despite her years of captivity by the order, but there was something dark and ancient about her and it made Fea's skin crawl.

"Well done," said the Mother, in the same flat tone.

"Thank, yo-," began the nervous Sister but The Mother's raised a silencing hand.

"For fixing the mess that almost cost us everything we have worked towards," she continued, each word like an iron spike being driven into the Sister. Both Sisters hung their heads. Fea smiled at their discomfort and the Mother turned her attention on her. "And you, girl. What am I to do with you?"

"My name is Fea. Fea Murrigan. And you can let me go, if you like, Mother," she said, in as brave a voice as she could muster.

A long silence greeted her comment, and Fea thought she'd gone too far. Then the mother shook and a strange wheezing noise that soon turned into a sharp hacking. Fea thought she was having a turn and her eyes instinctively darted towards the Sisters, searching for answers. They still bowed their heads in supplication. Then the realisation struck. *Holy god,* Fea thought. *Is she laughing?* Fea had never heard such an awful laugh in her life. She vowed to keep jokes to a minimum.

After the Mother's laughter subsided, she stood behind the desk and glided around to Fea's side. Fea swallowed hard. The Mother towered above not only her but the two Sister as well. *She must be seven feet tall,* thought Fea.

"You will stay here and work at the laundry, for what little time you have left," she said to Fea. "You'll soon wish that you took your own life rather than abscond. You won't get the opportunity again." She turned to the Sisters. "Find her somewhere to stay," she said. "She will work the steam room first thing in the morning."

"Yes, Mother."

"One of you will stay with her around the clock. I don't want her to escape again."

The Sisters nodded in unison.

The Mother turned from them dismissively; Fea's audience was over, and she was as good as forgotten. The Sisters took Fea's arms again and guided her out of the room.

ALONE ONCE MORE, The Mother folded herself into the chair behind her desk. The return of the Murrigan girl brought a wave of relief, and she was determined to keep a tight grip on her this time. Until the ritual was to take place. *Soon this will be over,* she thought, and a strange sensation came over her. Was it anticipation, was it nervousness? *A combination of them.* The order had never been so close to their goals' fruition. The Staff, the one elusive piece, was entrusted to the hound, who would bring it to her when the time was right. He was wayward, but he was also as efficient as he was brutal; a common trait of his bloodline and the primary reason for keeping him in her arsenal, despite the trouble he occasionally caused. A shudder ran over her body as she remembered the Sisters who had met their end trying to re-capture him on his last successful escape.

She was unsure of the precise moment when the stars would align for the ritual, but she knew it was imminent, possibly within days, if not mere hours. Until then, they would keep the Murrigan girl busy with the other women who worked in the hellish factory below. They had chosen this location for the laundry because of its proximity to the red-light district. In this place, heartless madams held captive women and girls, forcing them to work until they were discarded, ready to be claimed by her Order. Here, the misery would continue until the women released their last breath. Their combined misery sustained the Sisters of the Order and kept the gateway open for communication with those who waited. It was their only contact.

But all of that was about to change, and her former world was about to be made flesh on this one. The old gods would walk this earth again, and the insects that swarmed its surface would know their place in the grand scheme of things once more. And she would take her rightful place with her Sisters and resume the work that they had been charged with since time began. The Mother breathed a contented sigh. *Soon...*

CHAPTER 12

DOGFIGHT

Fiachra stood across the street from the expensive-looking townhouse on Dawson Street. He was certain the man he sought was inside despite not being able to sense him; the foul scent of magic overwhelmed most other scents, even with him only partially transformed and with the street between. This included the man and the finer details of his comings and goings, but not the scent of corrupted blood, which caused the bile to rise up his throat. "I know you're in there," he said, under his breath.

A lamplighter made his way along the street, lighting the gas lamps that lined each side. This part of the city was in stark contrast to Monto. The residents here were businesspeople and professionals, running retail establishments or offering services, as well as the wealthier class who used them. He noticed an abundance of police constables since crossing the river, with their whistles and truncheons at the ready for any trouble.

Fiachra attempted to blend into the background, sticking to shadowed doorways. The fading light made the task easier, but his loitering and his unkempt attire drew unwanted attention. He needed to clean up sooner rather than later.

Breaking cover, he walked across the road between two carriages with their curtains drawn for privacy. The drivers cracked the whip and shouted at his boldness, but he ignored them. On the other side, he adopted a casual gait and walked towards the building of interest. As he approached, the stench of corruption grew more potent. He exerted all his strength to ascend the steps to the front door.

Luck was with him; the door was unlocked, so he pushed it open enough to enter and closed it quickly after him. Once inside, the corrupt smell hit him like a wall. He doubled over and vomited. Globules of half-digested human organs splattered the floor with the bile. He felt better and stood, wiping his mouth on his sleeve. His eyes adjusted to the gloom when he allowed his wolf form to transform his vision. That other side of him was better at stalking through the gloom.

Straight down the hallway was the first dead one, drained of something vital and looking more like a century old, dried husk than a fresh corpse. The corruption was present, but was not overwhelming on this one. The intense smell wafted down from the stairway.

He ascended the steps, two at a time, more of the wolf form coming through. He paused at the top to sniff the air, then made his way to a door on the left. Pushing it open, he surveyed the scene within.

The corruption was a physical thing in that room, emanating from not one but two corpses. Both bodies were almost unrecognisable as being human, and both were far gone into decomposition, but he got the impression that they were not long dead. Judging by the clothing, the one close by the doorway had been a lady. A gentleman's corpse lay atop the desk at the far side of the room. He noted the rudimentary attempt at covering both bodies. *What happened here?*

Fiachra sensed the lingering presence of the man he tracked, or at least the power the man wielded. He couldn't tell where one began, and the other ended. *What am I tracking here?* Those bitches were light on details, and he might rue not asking them more questions. He had been so focused on getting away from his prison he'd not thought of why they chose him to track down what they'd lost.

Despite the strong residue in the room, the source of power was absent. He turned from the massacre and was about to continue along the hallway when he heard a sound from below. The front door opened and closed.

He stepped back inside the office and closed the door, leaving a gap to watch the hallway.

As Lorcan had approached his former home, the sight of his recent shame, the whisper in his mind, became more insistent. *Lorcan,* it whispered, addressing him by name now, *join with me and I will grant you the power you seek.*

It disturbed Lorcan that whatever entity this was knew him by name, but he guessed it plucked the information from his head, since that was where it lived. *If it exists as a distinct entity and not merely my own insanity speaking to me.* He, of course, had no way of knowing, but whatever the nature of the change that had taken him the previous night, he needed it again if he hoped to save Fea from the nuns.

"Are you alright, mister?" asked the girl, pulling him out of his musings.

They were across from his Dawson Street property, stopped on the footpath, causing a general nuisance to passersby. "What?" he asked.

"You stopped all of a sudden," she said. "You were whispering to yourself." The girl's look was one of childish curiosity, but it disconcerted him.

Lorcan hoped he hadn't been voicing his musings aloud, or worse. *Does that other voice speak through me?* He hoped not. "I'm fine," he said. "We're here." He indicated the house, and the children turned to look.

Tommy gave a low whistle. "That's where you live?" he asked.

"A long time ago," said Lorcan, without offering more.

"Are you rich?" asked Margaret.

"Not where it counts," he told her cryptically. He pointed further up the street. "I need one of you to keep watch from up there," and pointed back the way they'd come, "and the other keep watch from there."

"Can't we come in?" asked Margaret.

"No!" he said, with more volume than he'd wanted. "No," this time softly. "There are things within that aren't for your eyes."

The children looked at each other but did not press the point.

Lorcan crossed the street without looking back at them, trusting they'd do as they said they would. Trusting they'd do as they were told.

He found the front door unlocked, as he'd left it. He'd half expected the place to be overrun by the constabulary. *Can nobody smell the carnage inside?*

Within, he went straight to the stairs and ascended at a

brisk pace. No point in tempting fate and dallying longer than necessary. He rushed past his former office without looking in. He felt no need to remind himself of that act. Of those acts. After he'd passed his son's old bedroom and he'd started up the stairs to the second floor, he heard a door open in the hallway behind him. A quick glance over his shoulder showed him he was being pursued by a man-beast. *The monster,* he thought. *The girl spoke the truth.*

A boost of energy enlivened him, and he tore up the stairs and into the bedroom, leaping across the blood-stained sheets to the far side of the bed, where he remembered flinging the staff earlier that morning. For a heart-stopping moment, Lorcan couldn't see the damned thing, then it whispered to him.

Here... under...

It drew his eyes to the end of the bed where it met the wall and he saw the onyx handle sticking out, its darkness making it difficult to see in the gloom.

The door crashed open, and the monster entered, filling the doorway. It snuffled and pawed at its great snout before casting its golden eyes around the room and settling on him. Lorcan was sure there was equal parts wolf and man in the thing and a howl of victory solidified that impression. The creature bounded for him.

Lorcan dived for the staff and gripped its shaft. Turning, he held it aloft as the beast bore down.

FIACHRA CLOSED ON THE HUMAN, fighting against the stench of corrupt power that emanated from the staff he held. It almost muted the corruption coming from the man. Pulses of sensation hit him, distorting his focus, but he fought through it to get to the man. He knew he had to retrieve that staff. It was that which the Sisters sought; he was certain of it. *My bargaining chip,* he thought. *The key to my freedom.* "Give it to me," he growled at the man as he closed in.

The man gripped the staff in one hand and held his other hand up in a beckoning gesture. "Come get it," he said, in a voice that didn't belong in the world.

Fiachra thought the gloom must be playing tricks on his eyes because the man's features shifted, and a toothy smile became a nightmare vision. The man's pupils expanded into the whites of his eyes until only dual onyx globes remained.

With a roar, Fiachra leaped at the man and swiped as he came down. His blow took the man on the side of the head and his claws cut deep furrows into his cheek as he bounced the man's head off the wall. The man staggered but straightened, recovering speedily. *That should have killed him,* thought Fiachra, confused. "What are you?" he demanded. He moved in again and swiped upwards, slicing through the man's clothing at his belly and cutting four wide claw-marks. Blood gushed, the heady iron scent of it filling the room. The man fell down and crouched in on himself, holding his midsection.

Fiachra's keen sense of hearing picked up another of those disturbing whispers and the man rose to standing again. He turned to face Fiachra, and the wolf-man was astounded to see the wounds to his face knit together and heal before his eyes. The man's stomach wound mended itself, too.

Fiachra wasted no time, but rushed in again, reaching with both clawed hands to grab the daemon. *I'll cast him out the window if that's what it takes,* the wolf-man thought. But before he could touch him, the man had whispered something in a language that raised the fur on Fiachra's neck. Then the man softly touched Fiachra on the chest with his free hand and a pulse of power surged through him. Fiachra's vision darkened, and he fell into the black.

THE COLD SEEPED into Tommy as he sat atop the wall across from the house Lorcan had entered. The air felt like rain, and he didn't relish the thought. Neither he nor Margaret were dressed for a downpour. He glanced down the street and caught sight of his sister, but only barely, and then only because he knew where to look. A surge of pride filled him at how capable she was becoming.

He heard voices raised at a pitch that seemed out of place for the area, and he turned his attention back to his side of the street. *Fucking constabulary!* His eyes widened at the sight of what followed them. *Soldiers too! Jaysus Christ, what have I got us into?*

The police were in front, two uniformed men, one on each side of what must have been a detective. They stopped four houses up from the one he watched, and the detective kneeled in front of a young girl about Margaret's age, but far better dressed. A matronly woman stood behind the girl with a reassuring hand placed on her shoulder. Behind them were six armed soldiers, waiting for instructions from the lone officer.

They were too far away for Tommy to hear what the girl and the detective spoke of, but the girl pointed at the house Lorcan had entered a few minutes ago. Then she dropped her arm and turned to bury her face in the matron's legs. The woman comforted the girl as well as she could and led her away as the detective and officer bent heads together in conversation. With a nod, the officer directed the half-dozen soldiers in brown uniforms to move towards the house. The officer, detective, and two constables followed them.

Tommy whistled, and Margaret poked her head out. The boy gestured to the house as he hopped off the wall and ran to intercept the soldiers. "Mister! Help! Mister!" he shouted, and all eyes turned to him as Margaret slipped into the house.

"What is it, boy?" asked the officer, clearly irritated.

"There's been a robbery! I think they've killed some-one!" he said, trying to muster a couple of tears.

The detective shook his head and turned back to the house. "No time for you now, ragamuffin," he said. "One killing at a time. Forward, Lieutenant." The Lieutenant barked an order for the men to continue to the house.

Tommy gave it one last try, this time lurching in and throwing himself on the Lieutenant's legs. Too late, he recognised the man as the one he'd tried to pick-pocket a few nights ago. The one who had administered the beating of Tommy's life.

The man smiled a nasty smile. "Ah. Back for more, my little thief?" he said and pulled a handgun from a holster. The Lieutenant swiped at Tommy with the gun but only grazed the boy as he ducked out of the way.

"Enough of that, Lieutenant!" shouted the detective.

"I should shoot the little bastard for obstruction," said the Lieutenant.

"Leave the law to me," said the detective.

Tommy could only watch in despair as they descended upon the house that now held Margaret, as well as Lorcan.

He could only hope she had the sense to lead Lorcan out the back way.

POWER CONSUMED Lorcan as he flung the wolf-man across the room to slam into the wall close to the ceiling. The wolf-man then crashed to the floor, causing the wardrobe to fall over on top of him.

Destroy it... demanded the voice in his mind, but Lorcan felt himself on the edge of a cliff. If he didn't maintain control and prevent himself from falling off, Lorcan felt sure that he would be lost for good. He had to remain in control. *Be quiet, damn you,* he thought. *I have another use for you.* He felt light-headed and weak after healing himself, albeit with the aid of whatever entity was within the staff. He knew the object was infused with malevolence, using him as a conduit, just as he used it. If the wolf-man was still alive... Lorcan didn't think he'd survive another confrontation with the creature.

As he moved towards the door, he heard the splintering of wood. Turning, he watched with dreadful fascination as the wolf-man rose from the kindling that had been the wardrobe. For an instant, a bonnet that had once belonged to Nemhain perched atop the creature's head, reminding Lorcan of a fairy tale he'd once read to Cormac.

"I can't let you take it," said the wolf-man. He breathed hard, but took a step towards Lorcan, anyway. "It's the key to my freedom."

Lorcan pushed away the demonic presence that sought to control him but kept the staff up and at the ready. "I need it too, friend," he said. "Hard as it may be to believe, I need its power to free someone innocent from an order of immense evil." Lorcan raised his hands in a helpless gesture. "Evil to fight evil."

The wolf-man turned his head in a surreal canine gesture. "Order?" he growled. "An order of nuns?"

Lorcan lowered the staff just a little. *Could this be?* "Yes. Nuns. Do you know of the Sisters?"

"Witches, more like," growled the wolf-man. His face had become more human in form, and he hawked and spat a huge gob of wolf-phlegm on the carpet to emphasise his contempt. He gestured at the staff Lorcan held. "They're looking for that. Sent me after you to get it."

Before Lorcan's eyes, the remaining wolf characteristics changed into a man's countenance, only keeping the golden eyes which shone in the gloomy room. "Maybe we can help each other, brother," said the man.

"May-," began Lorcan, but the man raised his hand to silence him.

"There's someone below," he said. "Ready that thing."

"Lorcan," came a faint, panicked voice. *The girl!*

CHAPTER 13

SOLDIERS

Once the door closed behind her, Margaret found herself in profound darkness, unable to see her hands in front of her face. A vile smell assaulted her nostrils, causing her nose to wrinkle. She thought of Tommy. *I hope he's alright.* She knew the soldiers wouldn't care for anything a ragged boy had to say. He knew it too, but tried anyway to give her some time.

"Lorcan?" she called into the dark, a note of panic in her voice. As her eyes adjusted, she saw a hallway before her and a staircase to one side. Lorcan hadn't said where in the house he needed to go, so she was unsure of which path to take.

Even in the gloom, she could tell the house belonged to someone well off, and she wondered why anyone would want to leave such a place. She didn't understand Lorcan, but she thought there must be something terrible in the house to drive him away.

From above came the creaking of floorboards, so she went to the bottom of the staircase. She looked up, struggling to see into the darkness, then took a step back and stumbled over her own feet. She landed hard. Two glimmering eyes had appeared on the top of the stairs, attached to a shadowy shape. As she sat on her behind in the middle of the hallway, the shadow became a man. *The monster!* Margaret screamed as she scrambled to her feet again, heedless of her name being called.

"Margaret! Margaret!" said Lorcan, running from behind the monster and taking her in his arms. "It's okay, child. It's me, Lorcan!"

Margaret raised her hand, pointing a shaking finger at the monster that stood in apparent ease at the bottom of the stairs. "He ate Ratso!" she said in a small, trembling voice. "And the others." She buried her head in Lorcan's chest and sobbed.

"It's okay. He's with us now."

The calm of Lorcan's voice combined with his firm hold on her settled her nerves. She remembered why she was there. "Soldiers!" she cried.

At that moment, came smashing noises as booted feet kicked in the door behind them. Flickering gaslight washed over the two of them, Lorcan still crouching down to Margaret's level, with a hand to her shoulder for comfort. Margaret noticed he gripped the staff she'd last seen at the ash pit.

"YOU! ON THE GROUND!" shouted a soldier in the front. The rest of them filed in and surrounded Lorcan and her. They levelled six rifles and one handgun at them in their frozen tableau.

"What's the meaning of this?" asked Lorcan, keeping his voice steady and sure. He rose gradually so as not to spook any of the men. As he did so, he moved Margaret behind him.

"DON'T FAKIN' MOVE YOU CUNT!" shouted the commander.

"Let's keep things calm, officer," said Lorcan.

"DON'T TELL ME TO KEEP CALM," shouted the officer. Margaret thought his eyes might pop out of his head if he shouted any louder. Fear overwhelmed her, and tears welled in her eyes, blurring the men with guns as she peered around Lorcan's legs. She dared not wipe them away in case they shot at her. She looked to the steps, but the monster was nowhere to be seen. *Scared away like a little puppy,* she thought. She wished she could run away. Then she felt the fine hair on the back of her neck rise as if she were outside in a thunderstorm. There was a tingling sensation in her arm where Lorcan's free hand touched her.

"You'll do as you are told, SIR!" said a voice from above her, and it took a moment for Margaret to realise it was Lorcan. His voice had changed into something from nightmares.

"Suit yourself," said the officer. "FIRE AT WILL!"

The soldiers fired a volley, chambered another round and fired again, and again, as Margaret shrunk herself behind Lorcan. She felt his body shuddering from the impact of all those bullets. As each one struck, his hand tightened on her arm and the tingling sensation became more and more uncomfortable. She tried to pry his fingers away, but he was too strong. "Stop! Please!" But he couldn't hear her above the thunderous gunfire. As the tingling sensation intensified, her vision darkened, and she slumped against him.

~

As the soldiers stormed in, Fiachra backed up the stairs, allowing the darkness to enfold his transforming body. He watched from the shadows as the officer barked his orders at the strange staff-wielder and felt a begrudging admiration at his bravery. Shielding the girl from danger wasn't something Fiachra would have done. When the man pulled the power into himself, Fiachra had felt it just before its darkness overwhelmed his senses. *How can he stand it?* But when the man's face morphed into the grotesque, a pang of kinship hit the wolf-man.

"You'll do as you are told, SIR!" thundered the man, his voice echoing through the room. *How much of that is him, and how much is the staff?* Knowing the staff came from The Sisters, and the effect it had on his own abilities, made Fiachra suspicious. Fiachra was brutal, but in his mind, he was a creature of nature, albeit from a hidden domain. As he observed the power, there was a distinct lack of anything natural about it.

Riffle shots rang out, a deafening noise in the small hallway, and the man jerked as each bullet impacted. *That must hurt like a bitch,* thought Fiachra, not unsympathetic. In the last half century, he had firsthand experience of the sharp agony that comes with being shot. *At least they're not silver bullets!* Astonishingly, the man's smile grew as the bullets struck him.

Fiachra looked down at the girl who sheltered behind the man and saw her face contort in pain from the man's grip. Her mouth opened in a silent scream, and she said something inaudible as she tried to pry his fingers from her. Fiachra was sure something flowed from her and into the man through the point of contact. His yellow wolf's eyes saw her age visibly. *Impossible,* thought Fiachra. He was about to go to her aid, uncharacteristic of him, but whatever evil lived in the staff, he was sure harming the girl was unintentional on the man's part.

Then the soldiers stopped their barrage, and the man released his grip on the girl. She slumped forward, collapsing against the man. Fiachra couldn't determine if she still lived.

The man raised his arms and held them out to his sides, in imitation of the Lord on his cross. "For it is written, 'Vengeance is Mine, I will repay,' says the Lord." The man grinned like a maniac; his face distorted as though daemon possessed.

The soldiers looked from one to another, and even the loud-mouthed officer was stunned into silence.

Then the man's wounds repaired themselves, ejecting the twisted rounds that his flesh had just accepted. "You may have these back, soldier boys," a multitude of voices spoke through him.

"FACKING KILL IT!" screamed the officer, and the men fumbled to reload their rifles.

But the man seized the advantage. He rushed into the group and slashed the first soldier's throat open with a clawed hand, pausing a moment to accept the spurting fountain of blood. Moving to the next soldier, he drew a curved blade from the small of his back and slashed upwards, taking a portion of skull and brain off in a powerful strike. The section of skull spun into the air and the man batted it with the side of his blade into the officer's face. The sharp edge sliced the officer's nose in half, followed by the sound of breaking bone. A moment later, the officer dropped to the ground, unconscious.

The man's grin grotesquely widened, reminding Fiachra of the Cheshire cat, and the remaining four soldiers abandoned loading their weapons as they turned from the grinning maniac and bolted onto the street. He let them go, occupied now with the officer, ripping away his uniform to expose his chest.

Fiachra approached cautiously from the stairs and heard the guttural incantations as the man cut symbols into the officer's chest. The stone on the staff pulsated as his hands penetrated the officer's flesh. Again, Fiachra saw something vital flow into the man, this time from the officer.

While the man was distracted, the wolf-man gathered up the girl, an abandoned crumpled pile, and carried her to the kitchen at the back of the house.

TOMMY WAS at the end of his wits as he watched the soldiers kick the door down and storm into the house. *Please don't be there, Maggie, please don't be there!* He winced at each barked order from the officer and his heart almost burst from his chest when the rifles fired. Then quiet, followed by the sounds of chaos. When the soldiers ran out the door, Tommy released a breath he hadn't known he held. *Where's the rest of them?* He counted only four.

The two constables and the detective took one look at the fleeing soldiers, paying particular attention to the blood splatters on their too pale faces and uniforms, and they retreated too. Slowly, at first, but soon they raced the soldiers down the street.

As soon as they turned their backs, Tommy jumped out of cover and ran across the street into the house. He stepped across the massacred soldiers inside the door, scanning the area for his sister. "Margaret!" he called. "Margaret!"

When he spotted the daemon crouched over the officer, his mind flashed back to the ash pit and poor Katie. But then he took in the clothing that the thing wore and realised it was Lorcan. He had no sympathy for the officer, though. *Good riddance,* he thought.

Towards the back of the house, a flame was struck, and a lantern lit, sending a soft yellow glow along the hall to the entryway. He left the man Lorcan, if he was still a man, at whatever he was doing and moved towards the light. "Margaret?" he asked softly as he entered the kitchen.

Another man, a stranger to him, stood beside a counter in the centre of the kitchen on which lay the still form of his sister. He moved to her and touched her shoulder, shaking her gently. "Margaret? Are you alright?" There was no movement and Tommy leaned his ear to her mouth to check for a breath. Tears filled his eyes when he felt none. Stepping back, he studied her for any signs of life. *What happened to her face? She looks old.*

"I'm sorry, lad," said the stranger. "She's gone."

Tommy shook his head. "She can't be gone," he said, looking desperately at the man. "She's me sister."

The man shrugged his shoulders a fraction. "I'm sorry, lad."

Tommy checked Margaret for wounds, but couldn't find one. *I must have missed it.* He checked her again. "What happened to her?"

"I don't know, lad. It was dark."

But the man wouldn't meet his eye. Tommy swore they flickered to the front door and back again.

"Was it that... thing?" Tommy whispered, an acid hiss.

The man shook his head. But Tommy knew a lie when he heard it. Lies were the one constant in the boy's life. He looked towards the front door and saw Lorcan stand.

LORCAN SURFACED through a dense fog and the scene that greeted him made him double up and vomit on the destroyed body of the officer he still crouched over. He pulled his hand away from the chest and felt the tips of his fingers sucking as they exited the wounds there. He felt a sense of contentment from the entity in his mind and looked down to see he still gripped the staff in his other hand. Dropping it like it was a venomous snake from the depths of the jungle, he thought, *What have I done?*

He surveyed the damage, noting the other bodies. Their uniforms marked them as soldiers too, much like the man he was... his mind shied away from what he'd been doing to the body. *They were firing at us,* and with that recollection, he looked down at his clothing. He was covered in blood, and holes peppered his clothing, but his hands could find no wounds beneath the rags. *Firing at us? The girl!*

He searched the room again, more frantically, but couldn't find her. Then he heard voices from the kitchen. He stumbled down the hall and was relieved to see Tommy and the wolf-man beside the kitchen counter. Then he noticed the slight form laying there. "Oh, no!" he said. "Was she shot?" The memory came to him of moving to shield her when the soldiers charged in. *I moved her behind me and held her there when...* Memories of the barrage of bullets and his transformation flooded in. He'd been holding the girl as the staff flooded him with its power. It had pulled something from the girl to do so. He knew that for a certainty. "What have I done?" He sank down to the cold kitchen floor. "What have I done!"

He heard a hawking noise and felt a wet globule hit his face. "You murdered her, that's what you did," said the boy,

Tommy. Lorcan didn't move to clean the spittle from him. He simply watched as the boy reached around his sister and gently took her limp form into his arms.

"Do you need a hand, lad?" asked Fiachra, but Tommy shook his head.

Lorcan and Fiachra watched in silence as Tommy carried his sister past them and down the hall, into the dark evening of Dublin.

"I tried to shield her," said Lorcan.

"Aye. I saw you," said Fiachra.

"That... thing took over," said Lorcan, pointing towards the entrance.

"It's an evil, powerful thing," said Fiachra.

"What do they want it for?"

"The Sisters?" asked Fiachra, but didn't wait for confirmation. "For nothing good."

A certainty came over Lorcan then. "I'm going to use that thing to murder every one of them."

"Can't say as I'd argue with that course," said Fiachra.

"Take me to them."

"Aye, and gladly, but we should probably clean up first."

Lorcan nodded, seeing the sense in it. But his blood boiled all the same.

CHAPTER 14

RESCUE

Fea spent the rest of the day amongst the women of the Gloucester Street laundry. Little more than prisoners now, these women had come here by many routes. Some had been prostitutes, like Fea had briefly been, and they had run away from brothels or were expelled from them due to disease or age. For others, their families had considered some socially dysfunctional and committed them there with no hope of going home. Some were considered mentally deficient; some had been unmarried and with child. Whatever the reason they came here, they were all treated the same under this roof and spent their days doing penitence as hard labour, arms half boiled in vats of water as they washed the endless flow of linen that came before them.

The Sisters watched over everything and never missed an opportunity to abuse or degrade one of the 'children', as the women were called; they were all children here, whether young or old, and Fea soon learned that they expected her to call them 'Sister' or feel the back of a hand or the lash of a stick. Her back and the back of her legs were covered in a painful mass of welts from the long evening. The other women were silent though, like a building full of ghosts made flesh. *What have the Sisters done to them?* Fea's spirit revolted instinctively at the thought of becoming one of them. *I'll die first!*

She had always known, from her stay with them in their country convent, that the Sisters were not human, but she had seen such horrors that evening, horrors committed by the Sisters just to cause pain to one woman or another, that told her they were monsters too. They seemed to feed off the agony and terror they caused, and Fea sensed that was the whole point of this place, to be a constant waking nightmare, with no prospect of escape.

When the workday ended with a shrieking whistle blow and the women lined up mechanically to go to their sleeping quarters, Fea lined up too, but one of the Sisters assigned the special duty of watching her glided over and pulled her roughly from the line. "This way, child." She was to be separated from the rest.

Fea moved in the direction the Sister showed without a word. Her body ached with fatigue after pushing herself beyond her limits on an almost empty stomach.

"You have much to learn, child," said the Sister as she passed. Using the back of a hardened hand to Fea's face, the Sister knocked her to the floor.

The impact of hitting the ground sent a powerful shockwave through Fea's body, disorienting her for a moment.

"You will address me as Sister."

Fea slowly gained her feet. "Yes, Sister." She was too exhausted to fight. Her body needed rest. She trudged after the gliding figure down into the depths of the building to where the corridor narrowed and darkened. Small grates at eye level adorned the solidly constructed doors on either side. *Prison cells!*

The Sister stopped at one of these cells and opened it. "In here, child."

"Yes, Sister." She entered a tiny space with a bucket in one corner and a narrow cot to the side. The sound of the door slamming echoed through the room, leaving her with a sense of utter isolation. She sat on the bed and put her head in her hands, thinking of Lorcan, the one shining light in her recent life. She had no recollection of what had happened to him, but she hoped he had escaped and was far from these monsters. "Are you still alive?"

The sound of her voice echoed off the cold stone walls of the cell, creating an eerie, deafening effect, which only added to her growing sense of hopelessness. She lay down on the hard bed and pulled the threadbare blanket over her shoulders. There, her exhaustion pulled her into sleep.

THE COACH THUNDERED onto Gloucester Street at breakneck speed with Lorcan on the driver's board while Fiachra clung on for dear life in the cab below. A gentleman who nonchalantly crossed before the coach was almost pulled beneath the wheels, but a fellow Dubliner valiantly intervened and rescued him at the last possible moment. Lorcan cared not. He would trample whoever got in his way without a second thought.

Fire and darkness consumed him. Fire from the infernal flame of hatred for the Sisters, a brooding darkness brought on by his latest dark deed, the killing of an innocent child. He still could not quite believe that he had done it, and wondered if the force within the staff was solely to blame.

This is a cursed thing to be sure, but there's always been a darkness within me. Sure, hadn't father the same inside him? Lorcan suspected whatever entity possessed the staff had merely recognised his darkness and encouraged it to come to the fore. It provided an avenue through which he could tap into his personal dark force. *Well, I'm doing that with a vengeance now,* he thought. *For good or ill.*

He pulled back hard on the reins as he drew up outside the Temple Church. The horses neighed in protest at the rough treatment. The coachman must have had a gentle hand with the horses, but he always felt the beasts responded better to firmness. Lorcan had discovered the coach at the back of the Dawson Street residence, and they'd decided taking it through Dublin's streets was less risky than walking to their destination. Fiachra had initially protested but agreed for expediencies' sake.

Lorcan jumped down onto the street and opened the coach door. The pale face of Fiachra greeted him, the man making a hasty, stumbling exit. "For Christ's sake," he grumbled. "Was that yer first time driving one of these contraptions?"

Lorcan ignored him and reached into the cap to retrieve the bag he'd placed there. He shouldered it and closed the distance between himself and the Temple Church, following in Fiachra's wake. The man was already up the steps, between the pillars, and had turned the handle of the heavy double doors by the time Lorcan reached him. The doors groaned open, causing them to quicken their pace as they rushed inside and shut them tightly. Lorcan threw the bolt so as not to be disturbed.

"I'm sorry, gentlemen, but the Church is closed to the public until..." The man, a priest, judging by his vestments, had come from a door to the left. Upon seeing Lorcan's icy stare, he stopped what he was saying and took a step backwards.

Lorcan let the pack drop to the tiled floor and, with one smooth motion, produced the staff. Candlelight seemed to dim in its presence as though the staff consumed its radiance. "There are no gentlemen here, Father," said Lorcan.

The priest looked from the staff to Lorcan's too wide smile. He turned to Fiachra and saw amber, glowing eyes and a wolfish smile greeting him. The priest pivoted and raced down the aisle, past rows of worn varnished pews, towards the altar. His destination was the door to the altar's left.

His right hand grasping the staff's shaft, Lorcan raised his free hand towards the fleeing clergyman, and, with a quick flick of the wrist, he mouthed the word, "Return." A surge of power rushed through him, overwhelming him for an instant. He almost missed the priest rising as though picked up by an invisible hand and flung back, limbs waving about loose like a child's cloth doll, into the middle of the pews. The priest crashed down with a scream as his bones cracked and his muscles tore. His back bent over a pew and one leg twisted in an unnatural direction.

Lorcan thought the man was dead, but then came another agonised moan. He walked down the aisle and slid into the pew to take a seat beside the priest. Fiachra followed but stood at the end of the pew, still in the aisle, to observe.

The priest watched Lorcan with panicked eyes, not unlike those of an injured farm animal. It never ceased to amaze Lorcan how animals knew when they were in serious trouble. "Now. My questions," said Lorcan.

The minister opened his mouth to speak, but instead emitted a series of unintelligible groans.

"That's okay. No need to speak. Just blink once for yes and twice for no. I will help you if you answer truthfully. Do you understand?"

The minister struggled to move but tensed in pain. He focused intensely on Lorcan and closed his teary eyes for a moment, then opened them.

"Good man!" Lorcan shifted on the hard wooden seat, trying to get more comfortable. "Is there a lower level to this church?"

The minister blinked once.

"Through the door you were running towards?"

Another single blink.

"And from there, can I reach the tunnels?"

The priest's eyes opened wider and then darted around as if trying to escape.

"So you know of the tunnels, then? Good. How are they reached?"

The priest's jaw took on a stubborn aspect. He blinked once, twice.

"Now, now, Father." Lorcan reached over to the minister's twisted leg at a point where something sharp poked out of his flesh and into the cloth. A dark blossom had widened there. Lorcan steadied his hand with his fingers and slowly delved into the area with his thumb. The priest found his voice and filled the air with a chorus of screams. Lorcan released the pressure. "The tunnels, Father, and your pain will end."

The priest resurfaced from whatever pain filled ocean he was submerged in, focused watery eyes and blinked, once.

"Good. Can we reach the tunnels from the lower level through that door?"

A single blink again.

"Thank you, Father." Satisfied that the priest had told him the truth, Lorcan got up from the pew and walked towards the door. He then stopped having forgotten something. Returning to the twisted, helpless body in the pews, he drew his kukri and carefully cut the priest's throat. "There you are. Free as a bird, Father." Lorcan made wings of his hands and delicately fluttered them. "Fly away, fly away."

The priest's life slipped away, and his eyes lost their spark as his blood splattered in graceful arcs, staining the polished pews a more vibrant colour.

"You remember I told you where the tunnel entrance is?" asked Fiachra.

"Of course," said Lorcan. "But no point in leaving him alive to tell of our arrival."

Fiachra nodded. "True enough."

He followed as Lorcan led the way to the doorway and the Church's lower level.

Fea stood in a desolate wasteland, dust, and destruction all around for as far as she could see. She was on a rough, wide path and ahead of her were figures, travellers, all wrapped up in their own solitude. No one spoke, just walked towards an unknown destination. Fea shivered with the cold. She had never felt so alone.

In the distance, still many miles away, a storm raged. The storm headed in her direction, and it appeared to be engulfing the people on the path ahead of her. As it got closer, she made out shapes among the raging forces within the storm.

One of the shapes was unmistakably Lorcan. He walked towards her in the very centre of the raging storm and the storm moved at the pace at which he walked. The storm also contained other forms. To Lorcan's left side, a darkness floated. From this darkness, tendrils swirled away to consume, one at a time, the people on the path. It took something vital from them, and as soon as its touch vanished, the person it had been linked to collapsed on the spot. The handle of Lorcan's staff fused with the darkness, while its top emitted a pulsing glow for every new victim.

To Lorcan's right stalked what Fea could only describe as a beast-man. He walked upright, like a man, but his elongated and furred head had a mouth of jagged teeth. He voraciously consumed those on the path by opening his mouth impossibly wide and draining the same vital essence from their eyes and nose and mouth. The used-up husks were carelessly tossed onto the crowded path, littering the ground.

Fea was scared, made more so by Lorcan's ambivalence towards the actions of his ... his what? ... his companions? He kept his pace, casually stepping over the corpses falling before him. He didn't notice so intent was he on reaching her. She was sure that was his goal.

As if in response to her thoughts, Lorcan pointed towards her. His two companions paused for a moment to take her in and then all three attacked their task with renewed vigour, Lorcan increasing his speed and the other two doubling their efficiency at draining helpless victims.

Fea panicked, turned to run, but an endless flow of people walked the lonely path, and getting through them was impossible. She stumbled and fell, the mass of uncaring humanity closing the sky above her. They kicked and trampled on her until she felt completely submerged. She was unable to breathe. With one final push, she struggled to fill her lungs with the musty, stagnant air and let out a piercing scream, only to have it drowned out by the trampling footsteps above her. Spent now, *with all strength gone, she curled up like a babe in its mother's womb, closed her eyes and drifted away.*

"Fea."

She opened her eyes a slit and saw a path had cleared around her, filled with the broken shrivelled husks of those who had smothered her. The beast-man fed close by, as did the darkness, and before her knelt Lorcan, with a devilish smile and an outstretched hand. "We've come for you, Fea."

～

"Fea!"

Fea lay on the narrow cot and tossed and turned in her sleep. Sweat slicked her hair to her forehead. Still submerged in nightmare, she clawed the air, desperate to escape.

"Fea!"

She opened her eyes, feeling disoriented, not sure she had left the nightmare.

"Fea!"

"Lorcan?" Recognising his voice in that place added to her confusion.

"We've come for you, Fea!"

A foreboding sense of *déjà vu* spread through her mind. Surely Lorcan meant "I've come for you." Awake now, she sprang up and closed the distance to the cell door in three swift steps. She shook the door vigorously, the rattling sound echoing in the room. "Lorcan! I'm here!"

Footsteps pounded along the corridor outside, growing louder until they sounded as though they came from just beyond the door. *Is it an echo, or is there more than one pair of feet?* Her nightmare resurfaced, haunting her thoughts once again. "Lorcan?"

From outside, but not in a voice familiar to her, "She's behind this one." The sound of a body approaching grew louder, accompanied by the forceful pounding of the door from the other side. "Fea. Are you in there?"

Relief flooded her as recognition bloomed, "Lorcan!"

"Step away from the door."

She did as he bade and called, "I have!"

She wondered what he planned. Something strong enough to move the door would injure or even kill her. She panicked and cast her eyes about the room. There was little in the way of cover, except for the small cot tucked away in the corner. She lay down on her stomach and slid herself under as well as she could. She took a deep breath, preparing herself for what was to come, but nothing could have prepared her for what happened next. Where she expected an explosion, there came the screeching, grinding noise of twisting metal. She watched in awe from her vantage point beneath the bed as the door bent outward at the bottom and peeled up. The noise and slow pealing continued, and she saw beyond the door two pairs of feet, then legs, bodies, heads.

Lorcan stood there with his hand held out, palm to the ceiling being raised in time with the pealing door. He held the same staff he had held in her dream, the one with the darkness flowing from it. As her gaze landed on Lorcan's companion, she felt a surge of fear and had to resist the instinct to run. Behind Lorcan's left shoulder, as he had in the dream, stood the beast-man. His face was not as animalistic as her dream, but his eyes glowed in the poorly lit tunnel and his teeth looked sharp enough to chew through the door if he chose to. *What does this mean? Am I still dreaming?* She pinched herself until her eyes filled with tears, but she did not wake. The tears cleared as the screeching stopped and Lorcan entered her cell.

EXHAUSTED, Lorcan stumbled into the cell. Dealing with the minister and opening the cell door had exhausted the power stored in the staff. He had used up all of his own reserves, too. No matter. He had got to Fea, and she was alive, crawling from beneath the cot in the cell he had just opened, a look of mixed fear and relief on her tear-stained face.

She rushed to him once she gained her feet and hugged him tight. "I thought you were dead," she said.

He returned her embrace awkwardly, cautious of inadvertently doing her harm. He still held the staff in one hand and felt its hunger. *Feed me...* was a constant background whisper.

As she moved back, he released her with a hidden sigh of relief. She looked from him to his wolf-man companion standing outside the cell door. He wondered what she made of him; half changed as he was. "What is he? What are you?" she asked.

"This is Fiachra," said Lorcan. "He's a friend, and an enemy of the Sisters, too. He's agreed to help you escape."

"And you, Lorcan? You're escaping with us."

He shook his head. "No. I have business with these Sisters. And if they're not dealt with, you'll never be safe."

She said nothing. Made no move.

"Lady," said Fiachra. "We have to go. They'll be here soon."

Lorcan moved out of the cell, and after a moment's

hesitation, Fea followed. To Fiachra, Lorcan said, "You'll bring her back through the church?"

Fiachra nodded. "To get to the lower level of the Laundry, go through the door at the end of the corridor and up the stairway." He paused, then said, "I can come back…"

Lorcan shook his head. "See her safe." He produced the kukri from its sheath. "I'll deal with the witches."

He looked at Fea one last time, feeling an ache at the memories she stirred.

"Take care, Fea. Live a long life."

Without waiting for a response, Lorcan went down the corridor, the way Fiachra had shown. He wasn't one for drawn out goodbyes; they made him feel like a schoolboy. Behind him, he heard Fiachra and Fea move off.

Reaching the doorway at the corridor's end, Lorcan tested it and found it open. Two dozen cold stone steps saw him to another heavy door at the top. He gingerly pushed the door open and surveyed the large industrial steam room. The machinery had a life of its own, like he was in the belly of a colossal beast of fire and steam. He was alone there. *Where are they?* It was late; the darkness settling in, and he wondered where the Sisters slept. Did they need sleep like ordinary men and women? Lorcan didn't know enough about their nature to make a guess, and he cursed inwardly at that lack of knowledge. *What sort of half-cocked plan is this, anyway?*

As he crossed the steam room to a door on the far wall, he thought of Fea and that she, at least, was free of this place. Perhaps rescuing her would go someway to offset killing the child.

The far doorway wasn't as heavy, looking more like an internal door. He opened it and exited the steam room into another hallway. He crept along it, searching for where the Sisters might be sleeping.

CHAPTER 15
THE STARS ALIGN

The Mother sat on the cold, stone floor of the ritual chamber. Resting in her lap was a bowl of dark, inky liquid, its surface rippling as she observed the human cautiously moving through her domain.

The man's contorted features were visible in the small image reflected in the bowl, a testament to a power that exceeded the limits of his delicate form. Yet he clung onto the staff with unwavering determination. It never failed to astonish her how humans could defy their own rationality in pursuit of their goals. *Especially for the cause of vengeance.* Her mouth twisted into a cruel smile behind her mask. The stars shifted into place.

She touched the inky surface and caused a ripple to dissipate the image. Dripping more of her blood into the bowl from the recent cut, she concentrated on the hound. The image formed of him and the Murrigan girl exiting the tunnels to the Temple's basement. They slipped through the darkness, up the stairs, and into the church proper. The girl gasped when she saw the twisted body of the priest lying in a pool of his own blood from the gash in his throat.

She turned into the hound, averting her eyes, and because of that didn't notice the trio of Sisters enter through the main doors. The hound had seen them and walked to them, still holding the girl close.

The Mother's smile widened further. Her plans finally came to fruition.

~

FIACHRA HELD FEA CLOSE, his arms wrapped tightly around her, creating a sense of security. She was oblivious to the trio of silent Sisters, who stood mere feet away from her.

"Well done, hound," said the middle Sister.

He felt Fea tense upon hearing the distinctive voice of the Sister. Still clasping Fiachra securely, she half turned to look. "Sister," said Fiachra, and felt Fea release him and step back as though contact with him burned her. *No flies on this one,* he thought.

"No!" she said, her voice filled with defiance.

The pang of shame that washed over him took him aback. "Sorry, lass," he said. He shook the silver band attached to his arm. "You're the price of freedom."

The look of disgust she had for him was difficult to bear.

"He trusted you."

That one cut close to the bone too, but he gritted his teeth and pushed aside the shame and self-disgust, choosing to confront the harsh reality of the situation. "He hardly knew me. *You* don't know me." And it *was* the simple truth. He owed them nothing, and they should expect nothing from him. He knew from long experience that the only one looking out for him was himself. *Why does that look of her's sting so much?* Some part of him still cared. The other parts were getting angry. He grabbed her before she had the sense to run.

"Let me go!" she said, as she struggled against him, but she was no match for his strength.

Fiachra ignored her. "Here she is. The man, Lorcan, is still in there." He pointed back towards the tunnels beneath the church. "I've done my part. Now you do yours."

"Give her to us," said the Sister in the centre. She held out her left hand and the Sister on her left glided forward, towards Fiachra.

Seeing the Sister approach, Fea turned back to him. "Please, don't do this!"

"It's already done, lass."

The Sister glided over to them and took Fea's other arm as he released her into the Sister's charge. The betrayal didn't sit well with him, but he'd do anything so as not to be confined to that damned cell again. *I can handle the guilt until time does its work,* he thought. Time was good for that, at least. "Take this damned thing off," he said to the Sister in the centre, the one apparently in charge.

"The Mother will set you free," she said. All three of the Sisters turned in synchrony and glided out of the church. Fiachra had no choice but to follow.

Lorcan prowled along the poorly lit corridor. He checked each room as he went, but he had yet to find a single Sister. *Where are they?* He was eager to find them so that the infernal staff would shut up. Its constant staccato call of *Feed me... feed me...* inside his skull was driving him over the edge. "I'll feed you through the next window I come to!" he said, not liking the frayed edge in his voice. He knew it was an empty threat, and he assumed the entity knew that, too. He needed that thing if he was to have a chance against the Sisters.

He turned a corner and glimpsed black cloth, with a splash of white, vanishing around the next corner. *There you are!* He raced to the spot, quick as he could, but the Sister stood at the bottom of that corridor, impenetrable porcelain mask facing his way. He took a step towards her, but she glided away from him. Again, he ran to where she had disappeared. Two Sisters faced him when he gained that corner. He breathed hard from multiple bursts of speed in quick succession.

They didn't move until he took a step, each taking a different direction, one left and one right. At that corner, neither Sister waited for him.

Feed me...

When he chose the left-hand path, he was rewarded not by a porcelain masked Sister, but by whispers from the path he had taken. He followed the sounds to a doorway which opened to a stairway leading down into blackness. Looking around him, he spotted a candle. Sheathing his kukri, he grabbed it and spent a moment lighting it, then, with the staff in one hand and candle in the other, he descended into the darkness.

As SHE SAT with the bowl of inky liquid in her lap, the Mother waved away the image of the staff-wielder's journey through the building above. Standing tall, she watched as the Sisters entered the Ritual Chamber through the solitary door at the far end of the central aisle. They descended the spaced steps, accompanied by the hound and the Murrigan girl, to the dais upon which she stood.

Behind her, on the stone wall, was the gateway, another kind of doorway. The anticipation that coursed through her was so strong, it felt like a physical force. *A doorway soon to be open.*

The Sisters led the Murrigan girl to her. The girl had the audacity to glare up at her. There was no fear in her eyes, which irritated The Mother. "So glad you could join us, Fea," said The Mother.

"Go to hell, Mother," replied the girl, with an almost palpable venom.

"I would argue I am already there," said The Mother. She shifted her head subtly to indicate the altar, and the Sisters led the girl to the ordained spot. She looked to the remaining Sister and the hound. "As reliable as ever, hound," she said.

He pulled away from the Sister and moved rapidly to her, almost causing The Mother to step back. But she remained in control and at the last minute he stopped and shoved the silver bracelet under where her nose might be. "That one said you would release me," he growled, more wolf than man.

"Of course," she said. And reached beneath her habit for a heavy silver chain for just this eventuality. Before the hound realised what was happening, she had swung the chain around his body. Where the links touched him, his flesh seared and the smell of burnt hair and sizzling meat assailed them. The hound roared, but she pulled the loops of chain tight, binding him. He tried to transform, but so much of the precious metal in direct contact stunted his ability to do so.

"Nooo!" He collapsed to the floor.

The Mother savoured each sob, each tear, each cry. She moved to him and leaned over him as he writhed in agony on the cold stone. "Did you really think we would release such a useful creature as you, hound?" She shook her head in mock disappointment.

The hound didn't notice. His eyes locked onto the Murrigan girl, who met his gaze with a mixture of empathy and sorrow. "Forgive. Me," he said, each word on a separate breath.

"I do," said the girl.

The absence of any hint of malice in the girl's eyes disappointed The Mother. There was only forgiveness. *Time will tell if your forgiveness holds,* she thought. The night had only just begun. She clapped her hands and the door above opened again. The remaining Sisters entered and streamed into the stone pews to either side of the aisle. The ritual chamber filled as the Sisters from the laundry entered and occupied it. An air of expectancy permeated the room, creating a sense of anticipation.

Only one more piece remains.

CHAPTER 16
THE RITUAL

The passage went on and on. Lorcan thought he must have gone down three floors before he reached an ebony wooden door, banded in iron. He firmly pushed it and the solid door swung inwards without a sound. As it did so, the whispers he'd been following stopped.

The door opened onto a large stone corridor leading straight ahead, illuminated by rough-hewn torches in sconces along the wall. The corridor seemed carved from the very rock beneath the city. Alcoves, evenly spaced, lined both sides, each containing a grotesque, life-sized statue. What manner of creature they were Lorcan knew not, but he gripped the staff tighter and prepared to use its power should they move an inch.

A fine mist gave the air a hazy quality. The irritating smell caused his eyes to tear up as he moved down the corridor. There was no other choice for him but to take that path. After two score yards, he made out the dark shape of a double set of doors. Closing on them, he saw the doors were like those on the opposite end: heavy, ebony, and banded in iron.

He listened outside, but no sound came to him. He pushed, and the door opened into a large chamber. As he stepped through, rows of Sisters seated to either side of a central aisle turned their implacable porcelain masks his way. He ignored them. The far side of the chamber drew his attention.

Among the Sisters, one stood taller, dressed in white and wearing a black mask instead of the usual white porcelain. On a dais, she held a chain that connected to Fiachra, the wolf-man, whose face contorted in agony as the white metal seared his flesh. To one side of this strange Sister, two porcelain masked Sisters held Fea's arms.

"Lorcan!" cried Fea. "Run!"

He took a few strides into the room. "No," he said, and reached to his left for the closest Sister. As he grabbed her shoulder, he gave himself over to the staff, allowing the entity within it to take control. Guttural words he did not understand vomited forth in a voice he was becoming familiar with as his fingers dug into the Sister. He felt his stomach churn as an oily essence from the Sister seeped into his being. He gagged on the corruption, but it contained a heady undercurrent of raw power. Waves of pleasure coursed through his body, intensifying as the Sister's gasp transformed into a gut-wrenching scream. The Sister became drained and used up in moments. He moved to the next one and did the same. Within, a small part of him tried to raise an alarm. *It's too easy! Why aren't they resisting? It's a trap!* However, the entity disregarded his concern and effortlessly dismissed it, craving the next surge of raw power.

As he went from Sister to Sister, feeding from them,

filling himself to the brim, he transformed into a monstrosity. Appendages burst from his body, tearing through his clothing with a violent rip, as each of these winding limbs, hungry for more power, blindly sought other Sisters. And the Sisters accepted them. *They're sacrificing themselves,* that ever-diminishing piece of Lorcan thought.

When he reached the bottom of the aisle, a swathe of black robes lay in his wake, their shrivelled limbs poking out at odd angles. He had grown half again his size and was unrecognisable as human.

With great difficulty, he remembered what he was doing there and sought the girl. She stood between the two Sisters with her mouth agape in horror. Across from them, the white robed Sister stepped forward. She raised her clawed hand and a guttural incantation echoed from beneath her mask. Lorcan felt the pull of recognition, both from within him and from the staff. He had uttered similar words at the behest of the entity, and he had heard the language spoken what felt like weeks ago, in the ash pit dump.

The white Sister barked a last word of command and the staff raised up as though of its own accord. It pointed towards the onyx mirror hung on the wall and the corrupt essence recently extracted from the sacrificed Sisters flowed into it. The surface of the onyx mirror transformed into a gateway to an infinite abyss. Lorcan's stomach lurched from looking at it.

While the power flowed from him, the white Sister directed her attention to the Sisters holding the girl. She made a slicing motion with her hand. "Now!" Then she resumed her incantation.

Lorcan sensed the entity pull back, but try as he might,

he could not move. The Sister had somehow usurped control.

DESPITE HER INTENSE desire to scream, Fea's voice remained silent. She wouldn't have believed the twisted monstrosity before her had been Lorcan had she not witnessed his transformation with her own eyes. *What's happened to him?*

She didn't know how, but she had to escape this insane asylum. Testing the grips of the Sisters holding her, she found herself held fast. She had to escape this place and the abyss that had opened before her. She imagined a silence seeping from it that was deafening.

In an instant, the Sister on her right yanked Fea's arm forward and slashed open her forearm with a hand that resembled a sharp claw. Fea cried out at the unexpected assault, but could only watch helplessly as her blood arched out and flowed into the abyss beyond the mirror's frame. It swirled around in a hypnotic spiral as it fell into the vast emptiness. When she first saw it, she thought the decoration was strange and definitely out of place. But as her blood hit the surface and swirled into the mirror, crimson melding with black, something pulled at her mind. The thing had a dark purpose.

The swirling motion increased in speed and pulled the blood from her like a vampire, sucking it deeper into the blackness of the mirror. A wave of dizziness took her, and the beginnings of darkness edged in on the periphery of her vision. She didn't know how much longer she could endure, but weakness consumed her and held her captive. There was little she could do but accept her fate, the realisation sinking in with each passing moment.

From within the swirling ocean of agony, a thought surfaced in Fiachra's mind. *Fucking witches!* The silver chains seared into his flesh, taking off fur and flesh alike. It burned not only on the physical level but on the psychic level, too. He felt like his spirit was on fire.

Peering through slitted eyes, he saw the large swirling gateway fed by the evil power within Lorcan's staff, and the blood within Fea's veins. The girl wouldn't last much longer; she couldn't have that much blood within her slight frame.

The Mother had her back to him. At least for now, he remained forgotten by her. He struggled to a kneeling position, fighting through the agony. *Fucked if I'll die lying down.* He gained one foot... The next... *Fucked if I'll die on my knees.* He moved as quickly as his chained body would allow until he was at The Mother's back. She concentrated on her foul magic and didn't notice him... yet. Before she could, he swung the heavy chain around her neck and pulled backwards, using his weight to drag her to the ground. Then he jumped upon her, relying on his weight to keep her there for a few precious seconds.

"Lorcan!" he shouted.

A flicker of recognition and a brief interruption to the power flowing to the mirror.

"Lorcan! Free me!"

The monstrosity stared at him, its eyes devoid of recognition.

Fiachra showed the chains around his body. "Free me!" he pleaded.

A spark then, a twinkle of recognition, and Lorcan turned the staff on Fiachra. A blast of power like sludge on a coal face, like waste from the deepest latrine, hit him in the chest. The pain intensified for an instant, searing through his body like a raging fire, threatening to consume him and his sanity. Then, a soothing sensation of icy liquid enveloped him. Surprised, he opened his eyes and watched the silver chains liquefy and flow off him. Not only the recent chains given to him by The Mother, but the silver armband was gone too. *I'm free!* He thought and let out a howl of victory that echoed from the chamber walls.

Then he transformed into his full wolf form, no longer limited by the band they had forced him to wear. His body bulked out, his fur darkened and grew luxuriantly, and he stretched to his full height, equal to the large sister on the ground before him.

Without hesitation, before she could act, he pounced at her and snapped at her face. The onyx mask cracked and shattered, revealing the desiccated face beneath. Careless of what consuming the creature would do to him, Fiachra's jaws widened, and he bit down upon her, taking most of her face off to reveal bone, muscle, gristle, and brains that had no natural aspect to them. Half a tongue flopped around at the back where the throat began, but stopped after a final gasping gurgle.

WITH THE IMMEDIATE DANGERS ELIMINATED, Lorcan felt relief wash over him as his body returned to its familiar state. He knew the staff was on the verge of running out of power after using it to open the gateway and to release the wolf-man from his bonds. Seeing Fiachra take care of the white Sister, he turned to the two holding Fea. She was alarmingly pale, barely standing on her own.

He closed the distance between them and took hold of the Sister to Fea's left. The staff needed no encouragement in draining her. He turned to the other Sister, but she had already turned to flee, leaving Fea swaying in place.

Rather than pursue the Sister, Lorcan enclosed Fea in his arms and guided her to the floor. A quick look around told him that only Fiachra, Fea, and he remained in the chamber; the remaining Sisters had fled when Fiachra killed their leader.

"Is she still alive?" growled the wolf-man.

Lorcan moved his hands to her chest and felt life within. The slight rise and fall of her breasts matched her soft, barely audible breaths. He nodded. "Only just." His voice sounded alien to him, but he didn't have time to dwell on what that meant.

The sound of a hunting horn filled the chamber, and both men turned to the gateway. Something vast approached from the other side.

CHAPTER 17

BALOR AT THE GATE

"What is it?" asked Fiachra, in awe. Distance was difficult to gauge, but the creature seemed enormous, and it grew with each passing second.

"I don't know," said Lorcan. "But it's coming here."

A palpable sense of foreboding heralded the arrival of the entity. The gateway to the ritual chamber trembled in anticipation, a feeble barrier straining against the impending malevolence. The very atmosphere seemed to recoil as the colossal figure materialised, a monstrous silhouette emerging from the abyss.

Its towering form, clad in tattered, obsidian armour adorned with eerie, phosphorescent runes, cast a spectral glow upon the emptiness that surrounded him. His visage, shrouded in a grotesque mask of war, exuded an other-worldly dread. Unearthly whispers trailed in his wake, carrying tales of ancient horrors and unspeakable atrocities committed in the name of his dark dominion.

The ground of the chamber quivered as Lorcan and Fiachra, rooted in place, watched.

The entity's entourage, grotesque beings, twisted by the cruel hand of whatever realm spawned them. Nightmarish creatures with twisted limbs and gnarled features slithered and slunk at their master's side, their eyes gleaming with a malevolent hunger. A chorus of guttural growls and unsettling hisses echoed through the air alongside the deep call of the hunting horn, creating a cacophony that sent shivers down the spine of any who dared to witness this infernal procession.

As the entity approached the gateway, the air thickened with an oppressive aura, suffocating the very essence of hope. The gateway itself seemed to quiver in dread of the imminent invasion. The very fabric of reality seemed to strain against the intrusion, resisting the encroachment of the entity and his nightmarish retinue.

With each passing moment, the darkness seemed to deepen, the boundary between worlds growing ever thinner. The gateway groaned under the weight of the entity's malevolence, a feeble barrier straining to hold back the encroaching tide of darkness. As the dark lord reached out, a pale muscular arm attached to a hand with fingers like talons, the gateway wavered, its defences on the brink of collapse.

A chilling wind swept through the chamber, carrying the stench of decay and despair. The world held its breath, as if resigned to the impending doom that accompanied the ancient entity, the ancient god, a harbinger of nightmares that sought to eclipse all light and plunge the world into eternal shadows.

"We need to leave," said Fiachra. "Now!"

Lorcan stooped to Fea and pulled her into his arms, lifting her from the ground. He turned to Fiachra and thrust her into his heavily muscled wolf-man arms.

"Get her to safety," he said.

Fiachra looked at Lorcan, not understanding what he meant. The man had transformed into something unfathomable, but he was back to human form once more. Then the penny dropped. *He's not coming with us...*

"What will you do?" he asked the man.

"I'll close this gateway," he said, grim determination written on his face. He looked longingly at Fea. "If I don't shut it, she won't be safe. Make sure she lives a long life, eh?"

Fiachra nodded his enormous wolf's head. "I will." He considered Lorcan for another moment, then offered, "Good luck." He gripped the woman close to his chest and bounded up the central aisle, carrying her in a protective embrace as though she were a child. *This much I can do*, he thought. *And let the gods help anything that gets in my way.*

LORCAN WATCHED the double doors to the chamber for a moment after Fiachra and Fea had gone. Then he turned back to the gateway.

The hunting horn sounded again, a deafening wave. The demonic procession was almost here, the monstrous entity far too large for the gateway. Lorcan felt his mind stretch at the sight of the cavorting creatures accompanying it.

The Master... Lord Balor...

The knowledge came to him from the staff he held, and he recognised it as truth. And along with the knowledge came a feeling of kinship between the staff and the approaching god.

Lorcan looked down at the staff gripped in his hands

and weighed his options. "How about you join your god?" he asked. He didn't wait for an answer, but flung the staff at the gateway. It twisted end over end, heading for the middle of the opening, but when it reached the threshold between this world and whatever lay beyond, it stopped as though it hit a barrier. The staff dropped to the stone floor beneath the gateway with a clatter.

Not without you, brother... The familiar whisper in his mind. He swore it mocked him.

Lorcan approached the staff and picked it up again. It would have surprised him if it had been that easy to get rid of the thing. He looked into the gateway and felt the god's awareness of him like a freezing blast. The chamber reeked of corruption, but it held a strangely familiar scent. Gripping the staff tight, he touched his free hand to the gateway. It effortlessly entered, with the sensation of dipping his fingers into an icy pond.

The hunting horn sounded out again. The chattering of the entourage came from all around him. Much longer and the procession would be upon him. Already, the form of Balor filled the gateway.

"I mean, I was going to kill myself today anyway..." Saying that, he sensed panic, whether from the looming god or the staff. *Was it capable of such a thing?* He smiled widely and, before he could think much more about it, he leaped through the gateway, pulling the staff with him.

THE SISTER MATERIALISED from the shadows just as the hunting horn's echo dissipated and the gateway sealed shut. As she watched, the mirror transformed back into an opaque sheet of onyx, concealing its secrets once more.

Looking around, she took in the ritual chamber, and it's littering of dead Sisters. *So much pointless sacrifice with so little to show for it.*

The staff, which had served as a tangible link to their Lord in this realm, was no longer present. The Murrigan bloodline gone to who knows where. She looked at the mangled form on the floor. *The Mother, gone...* That last she could do something about.

She knelt beside the Mother's corpse and collected the pieces of her onyx mask, placing them to one side. Reaching up with both hands, she gripped her white porcelain mask on each side and pulled. It resisted, for a moment, then a moist sucking noise as her mask separated from her flesh. Beneath the mask, her face was twisted and ancient, covered in a dark organic substance. Her red eyes glowed. Casting the white mask to one side, she picked up the pieces of The Mother's onyx mask. She assembled the pieces, then brought them to her face. Nothing happened at first. Then she felt a tingling sensation as the mask glowed. Within seconds, the mask fused to her face, the separate pieces joining again with white seams. She reached down and took The Mother's coif instead of her own. It was covered in splatters of gore, but it would suffice until she found a pristine replacement in her quarters.

The new Mother stood up and dusted off her habit. It too would need replacing once she was in her chambers. She glided up the aisle, plotting and planning as she went. She would gather the Sisters who had fled and task them with cleansing the place. There was much work to do in preparation of the Lord Balor's future arrival. *I will be The Mother to usher him through the gateway.*

CHAPTER 18

ORPHAN

Tommy clutched Margaret to him as he walked down Mecklenburg street towards the flash house. He moved automatically, and only vaguely knew where he was going, his body acting reflexively while his mind was somewhere else. The few pedestrians who saw him beyond a dismissive glance, and thoroughly took in what he carried, gasped in dismay, but none stopped him or offered any aid.

Upon reaching the brothel's front door, he slumped down on the steps. As he cradled Margaret, his tears cascaded onto her, creating a pool of shared sorrow.

Behind him, he heard the front door open, and the harsh voice of Seamus rang out.

"Clear off, ya beggar, else I kick ye off!" A pause, while the brutish bully waited for his compliance, then a grunt of recognition. "Tommy O'Hare, as I live and breath. You've some cheek after the ruckus ya caused. Wait there!" The door slammed again as Seamus disappeared.

Throughout the one-sided exchange, Tommy didn't show that he heard Seamus at all. Each passing moment brought a fresh wave of sorrow, breaking his heart over and over again.

The door opened behind him, and soft footfalls approached. "Oh, dear," said Madam Arnott. She sat down next to Tommy on the step. "Is this your sister?"

Tommy nodded in answer. He felt the warmth of the madam's body seep into him, which only emphasised the coldness of his sister's.

"What happened to her?"

Fresh tears flowed from him as he stuttered his response. "The gentleman. Lorcan."

Madam Arnott was about to say something but thought better of it. Instead, she said. "Give her to me." She leaned over him, reaching for Margaret, and Tommy resisted.

The thought of someone taking the last part of his sister made him panic. He was not a fool; he knew Margaret was gone. But the only thing that kept him from losing his mind was the solidity of her slight form in his arms.

"It's okay, Tommy. We'll give her a fitting send-off. You have my word." She gently pulled the small body from his arms and this time, he let go. Madam Arnott stood, cradling Margaret's body in her arms. "Let's get you inside, boy."

After passing Margaret to the madam, Tommy felt his burden lift a little. He stood and followed the madam inside.

INSIDE THE FLASH HOUSE, Madam Arnott passed her charge to Seamus. "Lay her out in the first bedroom." She could tell by his expression he didn't approve, but she was certain he would do as she bid him. Tommy moved to follow Seamus up the stairs, but the madam held him back. "Let's get you cleaned up. Then you can tend to your sister."

Raising her voice, she called, "Jenny!"

In less than a minute, the housemaid appeared in the hallway, her apron neatly pressed and her hair perfectly pinned. "Yes, ma'am?"

"Please ensure that Tommy is properly groomed and dressed in clean attire. He will be our permanent guest, so let's get a room ready for him."

"Yes, ma'am," said Jenny, and led Tommy up the stairs.

A knock on the front door and Madam Arnott turned. With no one else around, she had no choice but to answer it herself. Opening the door, the sight of a man in work clothes met her. He fidgeted anxiously in front of her.

"Beggin' yer pardon, mistress. We 'ave a delivery for a Ms Madelaine Arnott." The man gestured to a cart on the street below, on top of which stood a large wooden crate.

"Ah, yes. I've been expecting it," she said. "You can bring it through here to the back."

"As you say, mistress."

She was about to turn, but she saw that the man had something else on his mind. "Was there something more?"

"Eh. The crate is moving, mistress. We was wonderin' what were inside."

The man's face turned red with embarrassment as he realised the enormity of the step he had taken outside his social station. The man's discomfort grew as Madam Arnott's blank stare met his question. She let the man stew in silence for a while before finally breaking it. "Bring the crate to the kitchen. I'll sign for it once you're done."

With a sense of relief, the man quickly responded, "Yes, mistress," before making his way back to the cart.

Madam Arnott studied the crate on the back of the cart,

her fingers itching with anticipation. If she was right about its contents, this discovery would secure her business's success for decades and potentially avoid a recurrence of the troubling events from the previous night. She was deeply concerned those events had cost her severely in terms of a trusting clientele. *Perhaps a new location is in order,* she thought as she went back inside.

EPILOGUE: THE END OF DAYS

Lillian held her breath, her body completely still, and focused the binoculars on the approaching car. It was too distant to discern any features, but she could tell it was a black car, possibly old-fashioned. *Isn't everything old-fashioned now?* What interested her was the enormous dark cloud of swirling nightmare which pursued the vehicle. *Maybe it only seems like it's chasing it,* she thought. Even though she couldn't hear the hunting horn or the screams of the damned, their echoes lingered in her mind. She shivered.

She heard Brendan approach, but didn't take her eyes from the distant scene.

"We have trouble to the east," he said.

"Johners?"

"No. That fucking shadow that's herding your collection." Brendan's voice gave no hint that he had once come close to joining her collection. It didn't surprise her. He was a man of few words, preferring to let his actions do the talking.

"That can wait," she said. She handed him the binoculars and pointed in the direction of the approaching vehicle. "We have a bigger problem."

Brendan focused in and swore. "For fuck's sake! Coming right for us."

"Looks like it."

"Huh," said Brendan, frowning slightly. He handed Lillian back the binoculars. "They've stopped."

Lillian accepted them and watched as two figures exited the vehicle, one tall, one shorter. The tall one opened the passenger door and retrieved something. *A child!* The couple and child started out on foot directly towards them. "We have to pick them up." She lowered the binoculars and noticed Brendan's questioning look. "If that thing is pursuing them, maybe we can redirect it."

Brendan was already nodding, a broad grin plastered across his face. "I know just the place to send it."

WITHIN THE SWIRLING cloud of nightmare, the Left Hand of Balor watched the family exit the horseless carriage and proceed on foot. He stood atop a writhing mass of Balor's minions, maintaining balance only through the staff's power. The same power kept the wailing shadows which swirled around him at bay. His long grey hair and beard moved as though in a slight breeze, as did his dark coat. His hand tightly grasped the twisted shaft of the staff, the sensation of its rough surface providing a sense of stability, as the dark stone at its top throbbed in harmony with his own pulse.

Soon!

Yes, soon. Was that him or the other? He could no longer tell where his own thoughts ended and the other's began. It felt like an eternity had passed since they first met. *No, not an eternity, but longer than the span of a single man's existence.*

Ahead, his quarry stopped. Another carriage pulled up in a cloud of dust and ushered them in. Then the second carriage sped away to the east.

The Left Hand of Balor pulled power from the staff and willed the immense cloud to turn in the new direction. He couldn't, wouldn't, let them escape. *Between them, they hold the key to my redemption.*

THANK YOU FOR READING

Thanks for reading Once Upon a Time in Monto. If you enjoyed this book, please consider leaving an honest review on Amazon, Goodreads, or wherever else you feel comfortable with. As an indie author, reviews are one of the best ways to raise visibility and slay those algorithmic monsters.

Best,

B.C.

RED JACKET: A PREQUEL TO SHADOW APOCALYPSE

Available to newsletter subscribers soon at www. bchollywood.com/newsletter .

THE DARKLE
CHRONICLES BOOK ONE

ACKNOWLEDGMENTS

I would like to thank the following individuals for their support and contributions to this project:

My family, for their patience and understanding when I'm spending time with stories and not with them.

My editor, Candace, who makes the invisible, visible, making the final project so much better.

My cover artist, Don, who takes a deluge of ideas and makes something cool with them.

My beta readers, Kate, Garrett, and Asia, who provided feedback and invaluable insights to help refine the narrative.

The readers (yep, you guys), for taking the time to read one of my stories for the first time, or for picking up another one. Without you, I'd just be having conversations with myself.

Thanks to all of you. You have my gratitude.

B.C. Hollywood

February, 2024

About the Author

B.C. Hollywood is an Irish author of dark fiction and extreme horror. He spends much of his spare time battering raw story ideas into shapelier form. He's worked as a milkman, a security guard, a waiter, a barman, a cinema projectionist, a photographer, a bouncer, and, more recently, various software related positions.

He writes novels, short stories, flash fiction, screenplays, and poetry. He is the author of *Dogcatcher: A Short Story,* the collection *Add me... and other warnings,* and *The Darkle Chronicles* series of extreme-horror, dark fantasy stories of which *Shadow Apocalypse* is book one and *Once Upon a Time in Monto* is book two.

To connect with B.C. and for news of his upcoming titles, you can check out his website at www.bchollywood.com, join his newsletter, and follow his Facebook author page.

The release of the third book in *The Darkle Chronicles* series, *The House of Marionettes,* is scheduled for the summer of 2024.